A Rex Graves Mystery Novella

PRELUDE
~ TO ~
MURDER

C. S. CHALLINOR

D1509539

First Edition

Cover art © Can Stock Photo, Inc., 2015

Book cover, design, and production by
Perfect Pages Literary Management, Inc.

ISBN-13: **978-1507764930**
ISBN-10: **1507764936**

PREVIOUS TITLES

REX GRAVES MYSTERY SERIES,
PUBLISHED BY MIDNIGHT INK
BOOKS:

Christmas Is Murder
Murder in the Raw
*Phi Beta Murder**
Murder on the Moor
Murder of the Bride
Murder at Midnight
Murder Comes Calling

OTHER REX GRAVES TITLES,
PUBLISHED BY PERFECT PAGES
LITERARY MANAGEMENT, INC.:

Murder at the Dolphin Inn
*SAY MURDER WITH FLOWERS: A Rex
Graves Mini-Mystery*
*SAY GOODBYE TO ARCHIE: A Rex Graves
Mini-Mystery*

~ PRELUDE TO MURDER ~

✳ ✳ ✳

"Love is poison."
~George R.R. Martin

~ONE~

At the end of Barley Close, one of the larger houses stood wreathed in police tape, the last thing Rex had expected to see on Helen's street during his weekend stay with her in Derby.

"Dare I ask?" he enquired, craning his neck from the passenger seat of his fiancée's car as she turned into her driveway.

"Dare I answer?" she retorted with a wry smile. "I was entertaining the forlorn hope that you wouldn't notice. Silly me! Or that the tape would be taken down before you arrived." She had just collected him from the railway station after his long trip from Edinburgh that morning.

Rex sensed her unease. After all, they were supposed to be discussing their wedding plans this weekend, and Helen wouldn't want to be side-tracked by his interest in a crime committed in her neighbourhood. "A burglary?" he asked with intentional nonchalance, getting out of the Renault and retrieving his suitcase from the back.

They walked up the path to her door, where she looked back at him before inserting the key in the lock. "Two deaths," she said and walked inside the 1930s semi-detached house. "A young couple."

Rex could barely contain himself. Two? And young? Unlikely it was an accident, then. However, he refrained from saying anything more and took his suitcase upstairs while his fiancée headed into the kitchen to prepare a late lunch. He continued to ponder the strange coincidence of two local deaths as he unpacked and put his toiletries in the bathroom. Two *murders*, perhaps.

Since Helen had not divulged further details, it was clear she did not want to discuss the event. They had postponed their wedding plans long enough, and their forthcoming nuptials were only months away. Helen had hoped for a May wedding, but had come around to a June one, to give their guests ample notice. Rex felt the customary jitters when he thought about the event. So much to do... Helen wanted a "proper" wedding. It was her first, whereas he was widowed. His marriage to Fiona twenty-seven years before seemed like a distant fairy tale. His son was now grown and pursuing studies in marine science in Florida. Rex sank down on the bed, holding three pairs of socks in his lap, and took a deep, calming breath.

"Are you all right, love?" Helen asked from the

door. He had not heard her come up the stairs.

He smiled at her. "Aye, it's just been a long week." He'd had a particularly arduous trial at the High Court of Justiciary in Edinburgh, so why would he even want to think about any more crime? And yet… He bit his lip and opened his arms to his fiancée. "I've missed you," he said, banishing all further thought of murder and marriage from his mind for the time being.

~TWO~

Helen had prepared a quiche, baked potatoes and salad. She had also prepared a folder containing information about their wedding, which they had decided to hold in the Highlands. They had gone as far as selecting a wedding planner by the name of Kirsten Abercrombie, who came highly recommended by one of Rex's legal colleagues, and with whom Helen had consulted over the phone.

They were to be married at Gleneagle Kirk and have the reception at Rex's country retreat, a converted hunting lodge. Kirsten had sent Helen suggestions for the catering, flowers, music, and all the rest of it. Just looking at the bulging folder on the table made Rex's head spin. He would have been happy to let Helen make the decisions about the table settings and other minutiae, but she wanted him to be involved in all the arrangements.

"All you have to do is say yes or no to the selections," she assured him, apparently sensing his anxiety.

"I see you've been busy," he said with an appreciative smile.

"And enjoyed every minute of it. I love the idea of a Scottish wedding, bagpipes and all."

Rex was privately relieved they would not be getting married in Derbyshire, where they had attended the fatal wedding of an ex-pupil from Helen's school. It had been enough to give even the most marriage-minded cold feet. By tacit agreement, they had not mentioned that murderous affair in the course of their own wedding plans.

He topped up his glass tankard with Guinness while Helen sipped her white wine across the kitchen table. "We'll get everything sorted this weekend," he promised. "And then you can let Kristen know what we decide and let her get on with it."

"Kirsten," Helen corrected.

"Aye, Kirsten. Anyway, that's what wedding planners are for."

Helen cast him an indulgent look over the rim of her glass. "I know how you hate all this, but it's going to be wonderful. You'll see."

"I know. But I'm more aboot being married than getting married, you know that," he said in his Lowland Scots. He raised his drink in a toast. "To my beautiful blonde bride."

"To my strapping, red-headed husband-to-be."

They clinked glasses.

"And I know you're just dying to ask," Helen said with an impish grin, "about what happened at the house down the street."

"Aye?" Rex said hopefully. "But it can wait," he caught himself. "Our wedding takes priority."

"I know it's going to be consuming you. I should have gone up to Edinburgh to stay with you instead, but I've got that meeting tomorrow."

Rex continued to eat and listened patiently while Helen explained the necessity of the Saturday meeting, some sort of intervention at a girl's parents' home. As a student counsellor, she had concerns about the pupil's suspected drug use. She sighed at length. "Anyway, as for Tom and Lydia Gladstone down the street, they'd been married seven years. They had everything going for them. And then *pouf!* Dead."

"How?" Rex asked.

"Antifreeze poisoning."

"Murdered?"

"That has yet to be determined."

"But not a suicide pact?"

Helen shook her head. "I just can't see it. They weren't found together; in the same room, I mean, and there's a young daughter, Hannah. Lydia's mother is taking care of her now."

"Any domestic problems?"

"Lydia, it seems, was carrying on with Tom's

uncle."

Rex paused in the process of dabbing at his beard with his napkin. "I see. Aye, that's a wee bit too domestic, is it not? Is Bob's-Your-Uncle a suspect?"

Helen laughed in spite of herself. "He's called Rob, actually. And, really, it's not funny," she said, straightening her face.

"When did they die?"

"Three weeks ago."

Rex thought for a moment. "You didn't mention it a fortnight ago when you were in Edinburgh."

"You were in the middle of that Ratcliff trial. I decided you had enough on your mind, and we have little enough time together as it is."

"You're right. So we'll not even discuss this Gladstone case," he said resolutely. "Although it does sound intriguing."

Helen laughed good-naturedly at him. "It's too much to expect you to resist. And it is rather juicy," she confided. "I even have a theory."

"Let's be having it then," Rex said in eager anticipation. "Just for the duration of lunch, mind. And then we'll go over those wedding details." He jerked his chin at the daunting-looking folder.

His fiancée adjusted her posture in her chair and pushed aside her plate. "Well, she began…"

~THREE~

Helen proceeded to tell him how she had attended a party at the Gladstone residence not long prior to her hosts' demise. They had just returned from a five-day trip to Paris and the festivities held a French flair, from the flowing Bordeaux wines to the delicate hors-d'oeuvres.

"Lydia had prepared some mini-quiches. I got the recipe from her." Helen gestured towards her quiche on the table, where only one slice remained.

"I take it one of the ingredients wasn't antifreeze," Rex joked.

"Nobody was ill that night," Helen informed him. "In fact, everybody was in really good spirits. Tom and Lydia especially. They were an extrovert and attractive couple, always the life of the party."

Until now, Rex thought.

"They were making jokes, a lot of French *double-entendre*, some of it quite racy. She looked lovely. The sapphires dangling from her ears were just beautiful with her dark hair. And he couldn't keep his hands off her. Mind you, he was a real flirt in general, but not offensively so. Good-looking too, a blond contrast to his wife, and almost as tall as you. Lydia was petite, even in high heels."

"How old were they?"

"It was Tom's fortieth birthday party. She was younger. Thirty-five, I think they said on the news."

"And the uncle? His uncle, I'm assuming."

"Right. Mid to late fifties. He owns the business they both worked for. He has a lot of money and likes to show it off. Gold Rolex, silver Porsche. Tall and nice-looking, as well. Receding hair, but still fit."

"Aye, I'm beginning to get the picture," Rex said. "Older rich boss; husband playing the field…"

"Tom? Not sure about that. He seemed devoted to Lydia and Hannah. He was married before. She was at the party. They had a son together, Hannah's half-brother."

"This just keeps getting cosier and cosier."

"Doesn't it though?" Helen refilled her glass.

"So, how did Tom and Lydia come to ingest antifreeze?" Rex asked. "And who found them?"

"The ex-wife, Natalie, came to collect the boy, who spent every other weekend with his dad. When no one answered the door, she walked in. The children were asleep on the sofa in their pajamas. She found Tom dead in the armchair in his study, and Lydia sprawled on the bathroom floor upstairs, unconscious in a pool of vomit. Tom had complained of the flu and had asked if Natalie could keep Devin that weekend, but she had arranged to go on a business trip with her husband. She called nine-nine-nine. It was late Sunday evening and suddenly all you could hear were sirens. I went outside to see what the commotion was about." Helen described how the SOCO team had descended on the Gladstone place and began milling about the property in their white bunny suits, arc lights blazing everywhere. The medical examiner arrived for Tom. Lydia was pronounced dead from a heart seizure soon after she got to hospital.

The doorbell rang. "I wonder who that could be," Helen said, getting up from her chair.

Rex listened as she opened the front door and spoke in animated tones to a female visitor. A woman in her late forties appeared at the kitchen entrance with Helen. Jill Nelson was a neighbour and friend of his fiancée's whom he had met before. She wore a seal brown jogging suit, her dun-coloured hair flecked with grey cut drastically short.

"Sorry to impose," she said to Rex. "I forgot you were going to be here this weekend."

"Join us for coffee," Helen insisted. "I was just

telling Rex about the Gladstones."

Jill took a seat at the table while her friend whisked the empty lunch plates away. "You didn't hear about it in Edinburgh?" she asked Rex.

"I didn't. Did you know them?"

"Not well, but we mingled at social gatherings in the neighbourhood."

"Jill was at Tom's birthday party too."

"That was a blast, wasn't it?" she addressed Helen, who was preparing coffee at the counter. "*Très chic* for Barley Close. The Gladstones were very up-and-coming," Jill explained to Rex. "I'm sure they would have moved somewhere posher eventually, but with Tom paying child support to his first wife, this was all they could afford for now."

"It's a nice enough house from what I've seen from the outside," Rex said. "Four bedrooms?"

"Yes, and very tastefully decorated inside. But Lydia was always hinting to Tom about moving to a nicer suburb."

"It's not like we live in the slums!" Helen objected. "I like my little semi."

"I know. What I mean is that Lydia had aspirations."

"Well, I can't argue with that. And they each had new cars. Hybrids. They were fashionably environmentally conscious."

Rex smiled as he listened to the women's

comments, which gave him an inside look at this perfect couple.

"And Hannah, their daughter, is just adorable," Jill gushed. "She said goodnight to the guests before Nanny took her up to bed. She looked like a little princess with her golden hair braided down the back of her nightdress."

"They had a nanny?" Rex asked.

"Not live-in." Helen returned to the table with a tray holding three cups and a fine china coffee pot decorated with bluebells. "She usually only worked weekdays. She stayed that night to help serve at the party."

"Had she been with them long?"

"A year?" Jill said, consulting Helen with a look.

"At least. She was young, maybe twenty, though seemed very competent."

"Pretty, but shy," Jill added.

"Still waters run deep. My theory that I was about to tell you," Helen told Rex, "was that *she* poisoned her employers."

"So she could get her hands on Tom," Jill explained.

"You share Helen's theory then?" Rex asked in amusement.

"It makes sense if you think about it. She spent a lot of time at their home, so would have known where the antifreeze was kept, and she was very attached to Hannah."

"And perhaps Tom," Helen added as she finished pouring the coffee.

"He was a catch. Almost twenty years older than Tracy, but incredibly seductive. He had these lovely dewy eyes. Hazel." Jill had clearly been smitten by her ex-neighbour. "And she definitely had goo-goo eyes for him. Wouldn't be the first time a man married the nanny."

"So why kill him?" Rex said, asking the obvious. "Or perhaps it was unintentional and she meant only to kill Lydia."

"We think it's because he refused to leave his wife, and Tracy was jealous of her. Also, some jewellery and ornaments went missing from the house a month prior to the poisonings. The patio door had been left unlocked. The police were called, but no one was ever charged."

"It could have been a random theft," Rex suggested, adding cream and sugar to his coffee.

Jill shrugged. "It was only Lydia's stuff that was stolen."

Rex nodded in thought. "That does seem odd. Did Lydia suspect her?"

"She never said so, and I expect the home insurance covered the losses, so she probably just went out and bought replacements. She liked to spend money, did Lydia. Oh, I suppose that's really catty of me, especially under the sad circumstances.

Sorry." Jill smiled apologetically.

"Well, it's true," Helen supported her friend. "But she and Tom both worked hard."

"What sort of business does the uncle own?"

"A furniture company," Jill answered. "They do those fruit armchairs and sofas. You must have seen them. I have one at home. It's a scooped out pear seat and so plush and comfortable. I love it."

"Fruité Furniture?" Rex asked. "Aye, I saw one of their round sofas in an art gallery, supposed to be a segmented orange or grapefruit."

"And they do interior banana hammocks for kids. So much fun. Wish I'd thought of it." Jill sighed wistfully. "Better than being a driving instructor." She ran a hand through her short hair. "Teaching teenagers to drive has turned me prematurely grey."

"No arrests in the case, I take it?"

Jill shook her head. "I'm sure all the family and friends have been questioned. Police officers canvassed our street to see if anyone had noticed anything suspicious that Sunday night, but nobody did. It's a cul-de-sac, so there's no through traffic."

"I can't see a stranger coming into their home and poisoning them with antifreeze," Rex said with a puzzled frown. "Did the police find any?"

"In the garage," Jill replied. "The papers said a container of coolant for cars."

"But their cars were almost brand new," Helen

offered.

"It was hidden, too. But that might have been so Hannah couldn't get at it. She's at that age, running around and into everything."

Rex asked about the antifreeze effects on the bodies, and the women relayed that the victims' skin had been pink and white, according to Natalie who found them. The ME had discovered oxalate crystals in their tissue. Both had suffered renal failure. Lydia's best friend, Cheryl, reported to police that when she had phoned early Sunday evening, Lydia's speech had been slurred, as though she were drunk. Lydia was known to indulge at parties, the friend told the media, but drinking at home when the couple was not entertaining was unusual.

What goes on behind closed doors…, Rex thought. "And you said Tom had the flu that weekend?" he confirmed with Helen.

"That's right. He mentioned at his birthday party that he'd been suffering from dizziness and abdominal pains, and wondered if he'd developed an allergy or stomach bug. His doctor was at a loss and was prescribing him medication that didn't help. But he said he felt fine that night and hadn't had any symptoms since before Paris."

"And how was Lydia?"

"In perfect health," Helen replied again. "She was knocking back the Absinthe they'd brought back from their trip, an aperitif she told us had been popular with Hemingway and Oscar Wilde, and Picasso, Vincent van Gogh, and other writers and artists."

"Tastes like Nyquil," Jill said with a grimace. "I tried it at the party. I don't like anything with aniseed in it."

"When was the party held?" Rex asked.

"In early February, two weeks before they died. Lydia threw it as a surprise for Tom's birthday. It was a Saturday."

"How many people attended?"

The women exchanged questioning looks. "About forty?" Helen answered. "Mostly family, friends, and colleagues, and half a dozen neighbours."

"Lydia went jogging with us sometimes," Jill said. "Slogging, she called it. That's how we knew her. She also did Pilates and hot yoga. She was really fit. The other neighbours at the party live in the bigger homes by the Gladstones'. It's shocking what happened," she added. "I don't see how their deaths could have been accidental, not when it happened to both of them. I'd really like to know for certain who killed them."

I would too, Rex said to himself, wondering if he would get the chance when he had promised Helen to dedicate his time to the wedding arrangements.

Jill politely declined Helen's offer of more coffee and said she had taken up enough of their precious time together. She got up from the table and bent to kiss Helen, and then saw herself out of the house.

"I see you've already been doing some sleuthing," Rex remarked with a smile after Jill left.

"You must think us a couple of gossips, but when it's people you know, you just can't help speculating, can you?"

"Understandably. I just thought you didn't want to discuss it."

"Not with you! I wanted to concentrate on the wedding."

"Well, let's get to it then."

They took the folder into the sitting room and made themselves comfortable on the sofa. For the next two hours they studied the information and made their selections, deciding on the menu and theme for the banquet. Helen's friend Julie from the school where they worked was to be her maid-of-honour. His son Campbell was to be best man. Afterwards, they went to the cinema to see a romantic comedy and then for a meal at a local Chinese restaurant. It was not until the next morning that Rex was able to further satisfy his growing interest in the Gladstone case.

~FOUR~

Helen had arranged to go jogging with Jill. Rex, meantime, decided to take a walk and, naturally, his morning stroll took him past the Gladstone house. The weather was mild for the time of year, no rain forecast, and he was in no hurry.

Barley Close consisted of prewar semi-detached homes by the entrance to the cul-de-sac where Helen lived. Towards the back, where the unfortunate couple had lived, the properties were separate and divided from each other and the street by low walls, their front squares and lozenges of lawn surrounded by shrubs and winter-bare ornamental trees. The victims' rectangular red-brick home, Rex noted, was spacious and well-maintained, but hardly pretentious.

The porticoed front door, coated with glossy dark green paint and fitted with a shiny brass knocker, flew open as he was retracing his steps along the pavement. A young girl with strawberry blonde ringlets turned to lock the door and then scurried down the path, carrying an object in the crook of her arm. Ducking under the police tape barring the gateposts to the driveway, she pulled up short in front of Rex. He had thought at first she might be the nanny going back to the house to pick up something for Hannah, but a closer look placed her at least ten years older than twenty.

"Hello," she squeaked, pale eyes wide with alarm. "Are you the police?"

"No," Rex said. "My fiancée lives down the street. Helen d'Arcy. I'm visiting."

"Oh, I know Helen. I just thought you might be from the police. You know, with your dark overcoat…"

And imposing height, he said to himself. "Rex Graves." He held out his hand.

Since she was clutching a book of some description in one arm and the front door key in her other hand, she hurriedly slipped the key into her jacket pocket and held out those fingers. "Cheryl, Lydia's friend. Best friend," she added, tears glazing her eyes. "Look, I shouldn't really be here. I best get going before somebody sees me."

"Where's your car parked?"

"Down the road." She nodded in the direction of the street entrance.

"I'm headed back there. I'll accompany you."

She fell into step with him, her blonde head above the fur-trimmed hood of her ski jacket barely reaching his shoulder.

"I'm sorry for your loss," Rex said. "Helen was telling me yesterday she attended a party at Tom and Lydia's last month. She sent a condolence card to Lydia's mother, but couldn't go to the funeral because she was at a conference in Birmingham." He squinted at the object in Cheryl's possession, which was likely the purpose of her furtive visit to the house. "Seems Lydia entrusted you with a key?" he said as he amended his longer stride to hers.

"I'd water the plants and feed the cat when they were away. I've taken Tabatha in."

"I'm sure the cat must be of some comfort to you."

"Paula—that's Lydia's mum—won't have a pet. She's very house-proud, but Hannah comes over to visit Tabs."

Rex gestured towards the item bundled under her arm. "Is that for Hannah?"

Cheryl did not answer immediately. "It's actually Lydia's diary. Thank God you're not a detective."

"Caught red-handed, eh?"

"I was hoping they wouldn't find it. How would you feel if some stranger's grubby hands were going through your private entries?"

"I'm surprised they didn't find it."

"It was well hidden. Only I knew where. Lydia

told me in case anything happened to her."

"Like what?"

Cheryl merely shrugged.

"I suppose you two didn't keep any secrets from each other?" Rex probed.

"For the most part," Cheryl said in a hesitant voice. "We were like sisters really. Neither of us had a sister." She stopped beside a white Volvo. "This is my car." She looked up at Rex. Her tiny nose, he noticed, was sprinkled with freckles, which added to her childish allure. "You won't tell, will you? About me taking this?" She nodded towards the diary. "Helen mentioned something about you being a barrister."

"Up in Edinburgh. Mum's the word, but if you come across anything in the journal that might point to a culprit, naturally you will go to the police…"

"You mean, like a clue? I suppose so. But then I'd have to tell them how I got hold of it." She looked at the exposed soft leather corner of the diary. "It has a lock, and I couldn't find the key. I'll have to break it open."

"Try a hair pin."

Cheryl smiled. "Well, it was nice to meet you." This me it was she who held out her hand.

"Likewise. I don't know if Helen also mentioned that murder mysteries are a morbid hobby of mine." He proffered his business card.

"So, if you do come across anything interesting… And only after you've gone to the police with it."

She nodded and took the card. "If you want my honest opinion, I think Rob Gladstone had something to do with it," she said, unlocking her car and getting in the driver's seat. "I thought they would have sussed that out by now." She slammed the door shut and started the engine.

Rex watched as she sped away. Deep in thought, he crossed the road. Cheryl suspected Uncle Rob while Helen and Jill favoured the nanny. No, he couldn't ignore the Gladstone case now. Family drama was fascinating, as long as it wasn't his own. How he wished he could be the one to leaf through the pages of Lydia's journal. Diaries held secrets, and the diary of a dead woman who had been having an affair? His curiosity burned to learn the truth behind the two murders.

~FIVE~

"It's an obsession," Helen pronounced over tea after showering from her jog and changing into a sweater and jeans. "Perhaps your mania for solving cases has grown worse since you gave up your pipe. It's not unusual for people to trade one addiction for another, you know."

Rex shook his head and smiled back at her. "I got the bug that Christmas at Swanmere Manor when, as you will recall, I was still smoking a pipe. I like puzzles, that's all."

Helen pointed a teaspoon at him from across the kitchen table. "You can't resist them," she corrected. "Well, if you can't beat 'em, join 'em, as they say." Her lips twitched in a mischievous smile.

He looked at her in mock dismay. "You mean you're going to help me try to solve this?"

"Won't be the first time. And we did make a lot of headway with the wedding yesterday and even got the guest list down to sixty."

Rex sat back in his chair and rubbed his

temples. "I kept dreaming aboot tartan napkins and floral arrangements last night."

"Good. That means it sank in."

They had planned a splendid catered banquet offering smoked salmon and roast beef, and sundry other delicacies, both sweet and savoury. But no cake. Not after that calamitous wedding in Derbyshire. A giant champagne sorbet garnished with exotic fruit would be their one deviation from tradition. However, they had failed to settle on an exact date, nor had they resolved the logistics of where they would make their home together. Helen had spoken about taking up a counselling position at a school in Edinburgh, but said she would have to ease into it. She was happy at work and would miss her friends.

"Would you happen to know how to get hold of Tom's ex-wife?" Rex asked, reverting to the Gladstone case.

"Natalie? You want to start with her?"

"Who knows someone better than a spouse? And who more likely to vent than an ex-spouse?"

"Depends who was responsible for the ex-ing, I suppose."

"My bet is on Tom. He sounds like a philanderer."

Helen chewed on her lip. "I wonder. And I wonder if he mended his philandering ways. I'm glad I don't have to worry about that with you."

She flicked a look at Rex. "I don't, do I?"

"You know you don't even have to ask, Helen."

"Yes," she said with certainty. "That's one of the reasons I have no qualms about marrying you."

"Nor I you. But if we are to be effective in solving this case, and it's a big 'if' based on the scant information, we must remain objective and not let our personal views colour our judgment."

"Of course not."

"Do you happen to have Natalie's number?" he asked as he pushed back his empty tea mug.

"I don't. I've only ever spoken a couple of words to her. But her husband's a dentist, and Jill is one of his patients. I can call her. Perhaps his practice is open on Saturdays."

Some minutes later, Helen returned to the kitchen after speaking with her friend. "Before I forget, Jill wants you to ring her. Something about a door-to-door salesman in the neighbourhood shortly before the Gladstones died."

Rex wasted no time contacting Jill while Helen went back into the hallway to make another call.

"That was quick," Jill said with a friendly laugh when he announced himself on the phone.

"A door-to-door salesman sounded suspicious. Was he selling encyclopaedias?"

"Vacuum cleaners, and he was very persistent. I bought a lithium battery-operated handheld just to get rid of the beastly little man. He saw my car's driving school sign and Learner plates and said it would be a handy little tool for cleaning. And it is pretty good, actually, though it only holds a charge for twenty minutes or so. Still, for thirty pounds I can't complain."

"You think he might have been casing the homes?"

"I don't know. It's just that we don't get many salespeople pounding the pavement these days, do we? And he looked a bit unkempt. Decent enough car, though. A Rover. This was a week or so before that event down the road. Helen doesn't remember him, but I think it was a weekday, and she would have been at work. Oh, and he was a Scotsman, but he didn't sound as refined as you," Jill added over the phone.

"Beastly wee Scotsmen forcing Hoovers on people," Rex joked. "Whatever is the world coming to? Did you mention him to the police when they canvassed the neighbourhood?"

"I didn't think to. I was in shock over Tom and Lydia's deaths. I was reminded of him earlier today when I was cleaning my car floor mats. Do you think it's important?"

Rex said he wasn't sure, but agreed it was a strange coincidence happening so close to the alleged murders, and thanked her for the information.

Helen returned to the kitchen. "I was able to get Natalie's number from the phone book. Jill told me her husband's surname is Purvis, but she didn't want to talk to me."

"What did you say?"

"I asked her how she was holding up, using the excuse that you had run into Cheryl this morning. Natalie said she was still in shock and couldn't believe her ex-husband was dead, and possibly murdered. I mentioned that you did a bit of private investigating on the side and might be able to help. But no luck. She said it upset her too much to talk about, and her son kept asking after Tom and what happened to him. He's only eight."

"Did she sound very upset?"

"More nervous, I'd say."

Rex stroked his beard pensively. "Looks like we're at a dead end with the ex-wife. Pity. She was the one who found the bodies. It would have been helpful to meet with her and get her perspective on things."

"As someone who knew the couple well," Helen agreed. "And the first one to find them dead…"

"Aye, and perhaps the last one to see them alive."

~SIX~

Failing Natalie, the person Rex next wanted to talk to was the nanny. Tracy had spent every weekday at the Gladstone house while Hannah's parents were at work and had helped out on occasion in the evening. She would know about the interactions of her employers and their routine better than most. In any case, Rex was loath to approach the victims' parents so soon. It had only been three weeks since Tom and Lydia died in their home. He really had no business poking his nose into their deaths in the first place, he reminded himself.

"Perhaps I should leave well alone," he told Helen as they returned from the supermarket that afternoon and began unloading the groceries from the car. Helen had been to her meeting with the pupil's parents earlier in the day, and he had spent time on the computer researching newspaper articles pertaining to the Gladstones' suspicious deaths.

"You mean, forget about the murders?" Helen stared at him in surprise. "That would be a first."

"It would. But it's not as though anyone has asked me to help solve the case in this instance." Rex lugged two shopping bags to the front door. "Perhaps we should just let the police do their job."

"They don't appear to be making much headway."

"That we know of," he corrected. "A lot goes on behind the scenes the public is not aware of. Three weeks is not a long time not to have made an arrest in a murder case. And it's just possible it was not murder."

Helen looked sceptical as she removed her jacket in the hallway and hung it up on the coat rack. "How do two adults accidentally swallow antifreeze kept in the garage? And, if it was a suicide pack, or even a murder-suicide, it's a bizarre choice of death, don't you think?"

"True. And one would expect a note," Rex said. "At least some instructions for the care of Hannah, if such arrangements had not previously been addressed in a will." No mention of a suicide note had been made public. In any event, he did not deem suicide likely from what he had been told about the young and vibrant couple. He took the shopping through to the kitchen. Upon placing the bags on the counter, he heard his mobile phone ring in his pocket and saw it was a local number.

"Hullo. Rex Graves," he answered.

"It's Cheryl," a young voice faltered on the other end. "We met this morning outside Lydia's house."

"Of course. How can I help you?" Rex calculated it had been about eight hours since their meeting, and wondered what Lydia's friend could be calling about, unless she'd discovered something of interest in the diary. Helen entered the kitchen at that point and he signaled with a raised finger that he was on an important call.

"I read the diary," Cheryl told him on the phone, confirming his guess. "I even missed lunch."

"That engrossing a read?" Rex said pleasantly.

"You could say that. Some of it, anyway. That part I can't repeat as it's private."

"Journals tend to be. How far back did you go?"

"It starts on the first of January of this year, which is soon after Lydia began her affair with Rob, Tom's uncle. Their first intimate encounter was at the company Christmas party. Then it was on his pool table, on the bonnet of his Porsche, and at various luxury hotels. I mean, she told me a lot of this stuff, but I can tell you, some of the entries made me blush. The man must have been on Viagra."

Rob Gladstone was not much older than him, Rex thought with a wince, which would have made him at least twenty years Lydia's senior. "Are you suggesting their relationship might have been the motive for Lydia's death?" he asked. Motive was what he was after, not the lurid details of an extra-marital affair.

"I just can't understand why she would take such a risk." Cheryl's voice betrayed frustration with her friend. "I mean, her husband's uncle? What was she playing at? But it seems she had suspicions about Tom's own fidelity."

Rex gave a sigh. "Oh, dear. And who might he have been seeing?" This was certainly getting complicated, he reflected.

"I don't know. Lydia never actually said anything about Tom cheating on her to me, which surprises me. I honestly didn't think we had any secrets from each other. We've known each other since our first year at Uni. Perhaps it was her pride that kept her from mentioning it, I don't know. But in the diary she writes about a change in Tom's attitude towards her. He was less spontaneous, she says, more tired, even falling asleep one evening as they sat together watching a true crime mystery on TV. One time she detected a whiff of perfume on his collar, expensive perfume, and he started taking longer than usual running errands or else picking up or dropping off Devin. But then they went to

Gay Paree and things seemed to be going better between them. She wrote that their passion was revived and they felt like new lovers again."

"I see," Rex said. "But was there something specific you wanted to tell me, Cheryl? Some clue as to how Lydia and Tom were poisoned, and by whom? Didn't you say this morning that Lydia had told you where to find the diary in case something happened to her?"

"Yes, she kept it in an antique writing desk that has a hidden drawer. But I don't think she meant if something happened to her in the way of murder; just that if she was run over by a bus or whatever, it was something she wanted me to have of hers, and of course, she wouldn't have wanted it falling into the wrong hands. Like her mother's. Her mum didn't like Tom much to begin with. If Paula had known about him cheating on her daughter, she would have told Lydia, 'Well, I did warn you!' " Cheryl imitated the mother in an unflatteringly common voice.

"And yet it looks very much as though she *was* murdered," Rex stated. "And that diary might hold vital clues. When was the last time she wrote in it?"

"The day before she, you know…died."

"Can you tell me what is says?"

Cheryl cleared her throat. " 'Busy day at the office,' " she read deadpan. " 'The brochures for the line of Very Berry Cushions came out really well. Daniel did a fantastic job with the lighting. Had lunch with Allison from Accounting. Rumour has it she and RG used to be an item until I joined the firm, but she didn't bring it up. T. is still feeling run down. Maybe he's getting too old and it's a problem keeping up with her.' *Her* is underlined," Cheryl informed Rex before continuing to read. " 'Hope he's okay for the big day tomorrow. Taking the kids to Chatsworth. N. is pleased because it's cultural and she's a Jane Austin nut. Can't keep my eyes open. Time for bed.' " Cheryl gave a sigh. "N is Natalie," she added.

So Tom was having an affair and Lydia knew about it, Rex reflected; though she didn't sound overly concerned. And what was the meaning behind the emphasized "her"? "That's the very last entry?" he questioned Cheryl.

"Yes. I imagine she didn't get the chance to write in her diary the next day."

"And Allison from Accounting... Was she a frequent visitor to the Gladstone home?"

"I saw her a few times at parties, but she wasn't someone Lydia saw a lot of outside work. Funny thing is she looks a lot like Lydia, but more exotic. She's of Indian descent. I suppose Rob likes petite brunettes."

"Who else is referred to by name or initial?" He sighed inwardly. So much easier if Cheryl would just give him the journal to read.

"Me, naturally, because we saw quite a lot of each other. Her mum, a few other people at work. The diary covers less than two months, so there's not that much."

"Who else at work?"

"David Lee. He's the chief bean counter. Lydia called him Bean Pole because he's tall, thin, and bald. He quibbled about the marketing budget. Nobody likes him. No social skills, but she and Tom invited him to some of their parties because he has clout. Married, three children. I don't think he's a person of interest."

Rex tended to agree, but wondered if Allison, who presumably worked under him, was worth talking to, even if she hadn't spent much time at the house. After all, she and Lydia had both been romantically involved with Rob Gladstone.

"Anyway," Cheryl interrupted his thoughts. "The reason I called is that there's someone who might be able to help us."

Rex was pleased Cheryl had said "us." It sounded as though she trusted him and they were officially allies. Meanwhile, Helen continued to put the food items away as quietly and unobtrusively as possible as he paced the floor, as was his custom while on his phone.

"And who might that be?" he asked Cheryl, disappointed that the young woman had not been able to extract more helpful evidence from the diary, but eager to hear about the new lead.

"Lydia told me about a psychic she met on the plane coming back from Paris, and she mentions it in her diary. She was going to consult this Madame Mathilde regarding her father, who died of a heart attack five years ago. Lydia wanted to make contact with him. She was devastated when she lost him so suddenly. Perhaps we could meet with Madame Mathilde and she could contact Lydia, you know, in the other world, and find out what happened to her."

Rex was beginning to see what might have drawn Lydia to Uncle Rob. A father figure, perhaps? And yet he did not feel enthusiastic about meeting with the psychic. Any psychic. "Ehm, let me get back with you on that. How do we know she's still in England?"

"She's here until May, according to the diary. She has clients in London and Derby."

"Incidentally, whose idea was it to go to Paris? Tom or Lydia's?"

"Totally Lydia's. She was so excited about it, and said she felt like a changed woman when she got back. Signed up for *cordon bleu* classes and was on her way to becoming a real Francophile."

Rex tried to think of something appropriately witty to say in French, and failed, his school *français* being woefully rusty. He said he would call Cheryl later that day or the next and urged her to think of anything else she might have read in the diary that might be useful in the case. Often, he told her, things later popped into one's head that had not occurred at the time.

"Any joy?" Helen asked when he ended the call.

"Cheryl suggested we enlist the services of a French psychic whom Lydia met on the plane from Paris."

"I can tell you're sceptical," Helen said with a smile. "But on the plus side, she had the opportunity to talk to Lydia. Psychics are intuitive, and if they met on the couple's recent trip to Paris, she may have picked up on something."

"Tom and Lydia must have gone to Paris to patch things up. Cheryl told me Lydia suspected her husband of infidelity on his side, while she was carrying on with Uncle Rob. But Paris in January is not Paris in May."

"Paris is Paris," Helen said.

Rex wondered if she might like to go there for their honeymoon.

Now that he was off the phone, Helen openly bustled about the kitchen preparing dinner. "Perhaps it was part business trip. But from what I could make out at the party, it had been more like a second honeymoon. They visited the Louvre and Versailles and strolled down the Champs-Elysées. Lydia enthused about the bistros and showed us what she had bought on the boulevard Saint-Michel in the Latin Quarter." Helen sounded wistful and a touch envious.

Rex now got the distinct impression she wanted to go to Paris for their honeymoon. "Aye, it wasn't a business trip from what I gathered. Far from it." He asked Helen if they were drinking red or white wine with dinner, and opened a bottle of Beaujolais.

"Well, if you do see the psychic, I'd like to be in on it," Helen said from the oven, where she stood stirring sauce in a pan. "Even if it's just for the entertainment value."

"Right," Rex said. "Not sure I could keep my face straight."

"Some people swear by them."

"The sort who swear they've seen ghosts and UFOs..." Rex held up his palms. "Well, who am I to say? Science has not fully explained away all phenomena. So, much as I prefer cold hard facts, I'll try to remain open-minded."

Helen cupped his bearded face in her hands and planted a kiss on his mouth on her way to the refrigerator. "That's very big of you."

"Anyway, it's not as though I have a pile of people to interview. The ex-wife won't talk. And I daren't approach Tom's parents or Lydia's mother in their time of grief." Rex poured the red wine into the crystal decanter he had bought Helen for

Christmas. "Cheryl said Lydia's mum didn't approve of Tom."

"Paula thought Tom was a womanizer. You just had to take one look at him to see he was a potential heart-breaker. And maybe she wasn't happy that he already had a child. There are often complications with ex-wives and joint custody. Plus Lydia had a wild side. Perhaps Paula thought her daughter needed a more stabilizing influence in her life. But I never saw her and her son-in-law on less than good terms on the few occasions I saw them together." Helen took the glass of wine Rex offered. "He probably won her around the way he did with all women—with flattery."

"Speaking from experience?" Rex asked, surprised to find himself a little piqued by jealousy. He didn't much like the sound of Tom. He'd known his type at university. They were part of the popular set and got the best-looking girls.

"He turned the charm on with every woman he met," Helen explained. "Didn't matter who or how old. I think he enjoyed his effect on women. Each conquest, on whatever level, probably gave his ego a lift, a bit like getting a fix."

Rex listened attentively. Helen had studied psychology and usually got a good read on people. That was partly why he valued her input on cases. "He sounds a bit shallow," he remarked as he leaned against the counter top.

"Narcissists are, if that's what he was. But by all accounts he was very competent professionally."

"What did he do at the furniture company?"

"Sales. What else?" Helen smiled and took a sip of wine.

"And Lydia?"

Helen thought for a moment. "Marketing, I believe."

"Do you happen to know any of their colleagues? An Allison from the accounting department? It seems Lydia replaced her in Rob Gladstone's affections."

His fiancée shook her head. "Sorry. I met a few of them at parties, but I don't recall any names. Allison doesn't ring a bell."

"Cheryl said she looks a bit like Lydia."

"Hm. I do remember a few young women with long, dark hair, though no one specific."

"She's petite," Rex supplied.

"And they were all petite. Perhaps Rob Gladstone employs a certain type of female." Helen halted her glass midway to her mouth. "Wait a minute. You could try Tom's younger brother, Daniel, who works at the firm."

"In what capacity?"

"I'm not sure. He'd hang out with the younger crowd. He's in his early thirties, unmarried. I don't know if I ever actually spoke to him."

"Close to his brother?"

Helen shrugged. "Hard to say. There was a large age gap."

"Other siblings?"

"None that I ever met, but I think I heard something about a sister living in Toronto."

"Think Daniel would talk to me?" Rex asked hopefully. "Does he know Tracy well?"

"The nanny?" Helen laughed. "Slow down, Rex! You're putting my head in a spin, and I know it's not the wine. I've only had a couple of sips. I can't get one in edgeways with all the questions," she joked.

"Sorry. I just get this tingly feeling when I'm on a case. I can't explain it."

"I can," Helen said. "It's your high. But with you, the case is your potential conquest."

Rex scratched behind his ear. "Not sure I like being psycho-analyzed. Or compared to Tom. But I suppose you're right. Once I get my teeth in a case, it's hard to let go, even though I was ready to give up on this one before Cheryl called offering her cooperation. And I'll admit I'm curious to meet Madame Mathilde."

~SEVEN~

As it turned out, the French psychic was unable to meet with Rex until the following weekend, and he planned to return to Derby then, much to Helen's delight. Cheryl had called Madame Mathilde to arrange the séance, and reported to Rex how upset the Frenchwoman had been to hear the news of Lydia's death. "So *tragique!*" Cheryl had mimicked on the phone. It seemed, however, that Madame Mathilde had experienced a premonition of impending misfortune when she had met Lydia on the plane.

Cheryl told him the psychic had requested a personal item of the deceased woman for the séance. Rex thought how macabre that sounded and began to feel slightly uneasy about the prospect of communicating with a dead person.

"So, what now?" Helen asked as they lay on the sofa during a commercial break in a World War II documentary on TV.

Rex knew immediately what she was alluding

to, since Cheryl's call had come just before the programme started.

"I thought I'd try to meet with Daniel tomorrow, unless you have plans for us?"

"Nothing special, and I don't suppose your meeting will take all day."

"That's if he gets back to me and accepts to meet." Rex had found Daniel Gladstone's number in the phone directory and had left a message on his home line before dinner. The young bachelor was in all probability out on a date.

As German tanks rolled onto the screen, Rex and Helen fell silent, but during the course of the documentary his thoughts reverted to the Gladstone case, and when his phone rang and he saw the local number he had rung earlier on the display, he jumped up from the sofa in eager anticipation. He took the call in the hallway so as not to disturb Helen. After listening to Rex explain his interest in the case, Daniel agreed to meet for coffee mid-morning the following day. Rex asked him to bring a photo of his brother. He had seen a couple of Tom Gladstone in the papers, but wanted to view something clearer and more personal.

He returned to the living room in time to witness shells exploding in snow and decimating the woods near Bastogne. Helen, who sat curled up on the sofa hugging a cushion, looked up and raised an eyebrow in question. Rex nodded with a brief smile. Now he would get to meet the younger brother. His private investigation was finally moving along after a slow start. Any qualms he had previously entertained about poking his nose into the local deaths were now buried. He was curious as to why, how, and at whose hand the glamorous couple had succumbed to antifreeze poisoning. But that could wait. He settled in with Helen on the sofa and made a conscious effort to ban all further speculation from his mind for the moment.

~EIGHT~

The following morning at the appointed time, Rex met Daniel Gladstone at Dilley's, a coffee shop close to the Fruité Furniture offices, where the young man said he was going afterwards to catch up on some work. An athletic six-foot tall and casually dressed, Daniel appeared shy, judging by his hesitant demeanor and half smile. Rex took an instant liking to him. He had Tom's large hazel eyes and chiseled nose, and sported designer stubble. Rex reiterated his commiserations on the loss of his brother.

As soon as they sat down in a booth, Daniel handed him a framed photo. "I brought this from home. I took it at my sister's wedding three years ago. She married a Canadian. That's Tom with Lydia, Dad, and Uncle Rob."

Tom Gladstone, strapping in build, was blessed with an actor's smile: A TV actor's if not big-screen, but enough to turn most women's heads. The male trio stood together in their tuxedos decorated with boutonnières and exuded confidence to the point of smugness. Tom resembled his dad, still a handsome man, though older than Rob. Lydia was visibly pregnant in a salmon pink silk gown. Her raven locks hung in sculpted wings either side of an oval face, her red harp-shaped lips suggesting a willful and possibly wayward personality. Here was a woman who knew what she wanted and intended to get it, Rex thought. He asked Daniel if he had been on good terms with his sister-in-law.

Daniel made a small grimace and ran his forefinger under his beaded leather wrist band. "For the most part," he said. "She could come across as bossy, but she had a great sense of humour. She worked in Marketing. I design the brochures and catalogues, as well as updating the company Web site, so we saw quite a bit of each other. Tom went to business school and I became a graphic artist. I'm, like, the black sheep of the family, not an A-type go-getter like the other Gladstone men."

"You enjoy working for the family business?"

"It pays the bills. I'd rather be taking photos of supermodels than pieces of furniture, but our product is more creative than most, so I'm not complaining. Who would've thought to make furniture look like fruit? Genius."

"Whose idea was it?" Rex asked.

"Lydia's, actually. Uncle Rob's been in the furniture business for yonks, and was producing mostly office stuff. Lydia had been looking for furniture for the house on Barley Close and said one night at a family dinner that modern furniture was boring, and why not introduce seating that made you feel relaxed and refreshed, like plunging into ripe fruit? Fruit has a subliminally health-conscious appeal. Uncle Rob thought the idea over and then asked if she would be interested in launching the new line. She helped design the prototypes. Fruité Furniture is environmentally friendly, all natural fibres and sustainable wood. For every tree we cut down, we plant a new one. And we use a lot of bamboo. It started out mostly as kiddie furniture, but developed into adult residential and commercial. It's amazing how it took off, and that's how I came on board. I was a struggling artist before then. Spent a year studying in Paris living as a half-starved bohemian, and decided the life wasn't for me, so this gig was a lucky break."

Rex nodded in understanding. Furthermore, he could see no reason for Daniel to bump off his elder brother and his sister-in-law who both indirectly contributed to his salary. Nor did the artistically-inclined young man seem as though he had the temperament for murder, though Rex knew all too well that appearances could be deceiving.

"Do you have any suspicions as to who may have killed Tom and his wife, assuming it was murder?" he asked.

Daniel shook his head, pulling back in his seat while a girl in a long brown linen apron delivered his green tea. She served Rex his coffee and hot cross bun. "Freak accident is all I can come up with," the young man said when she left the table. "Like I told the detectives, it's possible my niece poisoned her parents by mistake."

"Hannah?" Rex asked in surprise. "She's only, what, three?"

Daniel fiddled with his wrist band. "She has a plastic tea service and likes to invite friends and grown-ups to drink juice with her in her Wendy house. She might've found the antifreeze and thought it was apple juice or something. After all, it's green and tastes sweet."

"It's a plausible enough theory," Rex agreed. "But, if that's the case, it's lucky Hannah didn't drink any herself."

"Too right. And people don't always react to antifreeze immediately, so Tom or Lydia would've had time to replace it before they died, thinking maybe their spouse had used it and forgotten to put it away. I asked to borrow it once. It was kept high on a shelf in the garage, but Hannah is very nimble and incredibly sharp. She might have seen one of her parents taking it down. Most likely Tom, since he was handy with cars. Lydia didn't much like getting her hands dirty."

"Do you know if the police have questioned anyone particularly closely?" Rex enquired, stirring sugar into his coffee, while Daniel squirted honey into his tea.

"They questioned all the close friends and family members. Most had solid alibis, including myself. No one was at Tom and Lydia's house that night until Natalie, my brother's ex-wife, arrived to collect Devin. They were having a quiet Sunday evening in."

Since Rex was not investigating in an official capacity and didn't want to alienate Daniel, he refrained from asking where he had been, but Daniel supplied voluntarily that he was at a pub with his mates.

"What do you know about an Allison?"

"Allison Wilkins in Accounting?"

Rex nodded. "I'm assuming there's only the one Allison who works in the accounts department?"

"Yes, in receivables. I heard she and Rob Gladstone had private sessions in his office, and they were spotted in town together on occasion. This was before my time."

"She was Lydia's predecessor, so to speak?" This according to Lydia's diary.

Daniel squirmed in his seat. "I feel awkward discussing my late sister-in-law's affair, but, yeah, that's what I heard. I don't think Allison was heartbroken when it ended with Rob. She's engaged to a stockbroker now, a really nice bloke. In fact, they were at the Rose and Crown the night of the poisoning. Keith and I were participating in a dart tournament, which started at six. Allison and some other people from work were cheering us on. We left the pub well after nine."

"How were your brother and Lydia getting along, if you don't mind my asking?" Rex enquired, dismissing Allison as a crime of passion suspect, thanks to the alibi Daniel had furnished.

"Okay, I think. I didn't see Tom much outside work, except for family events. There's eight years' difference between us, and when he did pay attention to me growing up, it was mostly to bully me and play pranks on me and my friends. Once, he ripped the nylon strings off my guitar to use as fishing line. I was about eight and I remember crying. He backhanded me and called me a wimp. I kind of avoided him after that until he left for business school. He thought he could get away with anything, and mostly did. I don't introduce him to any of my girlfriends now because he's such a flirt and likes goading me."

In using the present tense, Daniel appeared to have forgotten his brother was dead. His fists balled tight on the table, while a bitter smile registered on his face. "He had to prove to himself he could get any female who walked within his line of vision, even if she belonged to me."

"I hope he showed more tact in front of Lydia," Rex observed, tearing his bun apart.

"Yeah. Maybe. Not sure she would have put up with it. Of course, her fling with my uncle could've been a way to get back at him. A huge slap in the face, that was."

"You say 'fling.' It wasn't anything serious?"

Daniel looked stunned, and then amused. "I wouldn't have thought so. I mean, the bloke's fifty-six. I know he thinks he's all that and throws money about like confetti, but, no, I doubt it was serious." Daniel chuckled wryly. "My dad went ballistic when he found out. Of course both Rob and Lydia denied it and said they were just working late on project deadlines. Dad told Tom to pay more attention to his wife or it would end up costing him dearly in a second divorce. I think that's what Paris was all about. They went there a few weeks before they died, ironically enough."

Or not so ironic, Rex thought.

"Look, I know what you said on the phone about sidelining in murder cases, but why the interest in ours? If it was murder…intentional, I mean, and not an accident?"

"My fiancée knew them. She went jogging with

Lydia. Helen. Helen d'Arcy."

Daniel continued to look vacant, so Rex whipped out his wallet and showed him a snapshot of his fiancée. He also pulled out enough money to cover the bill.

"Oh, yes, I do know her. I mean, I've seen her a few times at their place." Daniel checked his phone. "I should get going, unless there was anything else you wanted to ask me?"

"No, not for now, anyway. And thanks a lot."

"No problem. Hope you solve the case. You've got my card, yeah? Just call if you need me."

"There is one other thing, actually," Rex said as they both rose from the table. "Do you have the nanny's number?"

"Tracy's?" The young man shook his head slowly. "I don't. I didn't know her that well."

They parted outside Dilley's, and Rex sauntered down the High Street in search of a newsagent's. He found one that sold humbugs, his sweet of choice since he had stopped smoking his pipe. Untwisting the wrapper, he popped the brown-striped confection into his mouth, savouring the peppermint taste of the shell before crunching through to the chewy centre. He spotted a florist and on impulse decided to buy a bouquet of pink and yellow roses for Helen. She truly was a patient woman, he thought with gratitude as he regained the Renault. An independent woman with many friends and varied interests, she did not place undue demands on his time or nag him about his fascination with murder cases. Carefully placing the flowers on the passenger seat, he eased out of the parking space and drove back to Barley Close in a content and carefree mood.

Helen had not yet returned from her shopping trip to Westfield with her friend Julie from the school, so he put the roses in a vase of water and placed them on the kitchen table. While he awaited her return in the sitting room, he made notes in his legal pad under a section entitled, "Gladstone Case." He recorded the resentment displayed by Daniel towards Tom, his apparently neutral feelings about Lydia, and how he suspected Hannah of playing with the antifreeze. When he later told Helen about Daniel's tea party theory, she asked if antifreeze had been found in the toy cups.

"I didn't see anything about that in the newspaper articles or on the news," she said. She deposited her purchases on the rug and took a seat beside Rex on the sofa.

"Nor I, but does that seem to you like a plausible explanation for the double poisoning?" Rex asked. "Or was Hannah helped along by an adult? The antifreeze may have been administered over a period of time in Tom's case, the cause of his mysterious illness, with a fatal dose at the end, which knocked out both parents at the same time. There's been no mention of Lydia getting ill prior to that."

"Devin could've just as easily put the antifreeze somewhere he shouldn't. He's eight, after all, and could have climbed up the shelf in the garage. And he was staying the weekend, wasn't he?"

"I'd forgotten aboot the lad, but aye, Natalie came to get him, didn't she? That's when she found the bodies. What if she suspected what had happened and rinsed out the cups before the police arrived? Perhaps that's why she was reluctant to talk to us, because she was protecting her son."

Helen shrugged and nodded. "That sounds plausible. There was nobody else in the house that evening apart from the family."

"That we know of. Tracy wasn't usually there on weekends. But a friend or family member could have popped by unnoticed by neighbours and not told the police. Perhaps they're going with Daniel's explanation that Hannah, or perhaps Devin, inadvertently poisoned their father and Lydia."

Helen pulled in her lips and thought for a moment. "What if Natalie didn't want to share custody of Devin and wanted revenge on her cheating ex and his new wife?"

"I know I called him a philanderer, but do we know for a fact he left her, and not the other way round?" Rex asked. "After all, she remarried and was on decent terms with them both—enough, anyway, to attend their parties."

"Funny how well everybody got on with each other, isn't it?" Helen remarked. "But perhaps they put on a brave face for the sake of the children. What did you make of Daniel? Nice-looking young man, don't you think? Doesn't have his brother's panache, though. Tom sort of eclipsed everybody when he was in the room. I wonder if Daniel resented it."

"I can't say he seemed devastated over his brother's loss. Or Lydia's. But he came across as helpful. I liked him."

Helen rose from the sofa and picked up her bags. "I'll just hang up these clothes in the bedroom and I'll be right down."

"Did you get anything nice?" Rex asked, which he had to admit to himself was a nonsensical question, but he wanted to show interest and not seem as though he were completely consumed by the case.

"Actually, yes. There was a sale at Debenhams. Julie made out like a bandit. And I may have found the perfect wedding dress." Helen smiled and winked at him.

"Cause for celebration." Rex suggested they go out for a pub lunch in one of the neighbouring villages and take a long walk in the countryside afterwards. The rain had held off, which was unusual for March. The rest of the day he would stay off the case. In any event, there was no one left to interview until he met with Madame Mathilde the following weekend, and he had gleaned everything he possibly could online. He even resisted calling Cheryl to see if she had turned up anything new in Lydia's diary.

He would be seeing her next Saturday at the séance. She was desperate to find out what had happened to her late friend, as was he, and he was happy to pay the psychic her exorbitant fee. He began to look forward to the séance with much anticipation, along with a liberal dose of scepticism. Helen said at the very least it could be a hoot.

~NINE~

Rex was busy at the High Court of Justiciary in Edinburgh during the week and consistently worked late in his chambers, not returning to his mother's house in Morningside much before dinner time. After the meal, he would put in another hour or so of work on the documents he had brought home with him, and was thus able to clear his desk of the most urgent matters by Friday afternoon and catch the train back to Derby.

Helen was waiting for him at the brightly lit Derby Midland Station wearing black leather boots beneath her tightly cinched raincoat. She beamed when she saw him enter the terminal.

"Right on time!" she exclaimed as she hugged him. "You must be famished."

They decided to go to a popular steakhouse close by in the city. "Did you have a good day?" she asked.

"Aye. Alistair sends his best." Alistair Frazer was a legal colleague and close friend. "He wanted to know if we've set the date for the big day."

"Something we should try to settle on this weekend," Helen said as they walked to the parking lot.

The following evening, Rex waited with Helen in her living room for Cheryl and Madame Mathilde, who were due to arrive at six. He paced the carpet and thumbed the bowl of the pipe buried in his jacket pocket, a soothing mechanism he had adopted since he stopped smoking.

"Sit down and have some wine," Helen remonstrated. "You're making me nervous. She rearranged the pink and yellow roses on the coffee table. "These haven't lost their bloom since last weekend."

"Madame Mathilde sounded a bit flighty on the phone. I'm worried she might cancel at the last moment."

"It is the last moment, just about," Helen told him. "It's five to six."

Rex glanced at the mantelpiece, but couldn't help consulting his watch to make sure the carriage clock showed the correct time. At that moment the sound of a car slowing in the street in front of the house sent him striding to the bay window. "It's Cheryl," he announced, seeing her white Volvo.

Helen got up from the sofa to greet the young woman at the door. Rex heard amiable chatter in the hallway, and then Helen reappeared with their first guest, who carried a shiny red gift bag. He smiled and said hello while Helen poured a glass of wine and handed it to Cheryl.

"Thanks, I really need this," the younger blonde said, accepting the drink. "I so want to make contact with Lydia, but at the same time I'm scared to death."

"I know what you mean," Helen said, conducting her to the sofa. "That's lovely perfume you're wearing."

"It's *Joie de vivre*, Lydia's favourite."

"Joy of living," Helen murmured to herself. "How tragically ironic."

"I wear it to remember her by."

"Our Gallic psychic is late," Rex declared from the window in a displeased tone. He highly valued punctuality and didn't see that mediums should be excused, even if they could transcend time and space. "Wait," he said. "She just pulled up in a Jag. She must be quite good at her job. I suppose we'll know soon enough." But at least she had met Lydia and might have something useful to contribute from her ordinary powers of observation.

Cheryl clenched her hands in her lap. "I think I'm going to be sick," she mumbled.

While Helen consoled her, Rex went to answer the door. He had expected a gypsy-type woman and was not disappointed, except that this psychic was well-heeled and *soignée*: Abundant dark hair to her shoulders that was glamorously streaked with silver, dangling jade stones in her ears, and eyes matching in colour… They exchanged pleasantries as he took her expensive faux fur coat. A silk scarf in myriad shades of green draped the shoulders of her black dress.

"This way," he invited, leading her into the sitting room in front of the curious gazes of the two women on the sofa. She exclaimed in delight upon seeing the roses. Rex made the introductions.

Helen, remembering her manners, jumped up and extended her hand. "*Enchantée*," she greeted the psychic.

"*Ah, vous parlez français?*" Madame Mathilde said in polite surprise.

"*J'essaie*," Helen replied modestly. In reality, her French was quite good, as Rex had discovered early on in their relationship.

The psychic turned to the younger woman. "You must be Cheryl," she said, whether by deduction or divination, and pronouncing her name as *Shereel*.

"So glad you agreed to come," Cheryl said with a slight stammer and looking a wee bit pale, Rex thought.

"*Venez*," Madame Mathilde said kindly. "There is no need to be nervous." She had perfect diction, with a distinct French accent. "You are Lydia's dearest friend. You have nothing to fear from her spirit if she chooses to communicate with us."

"I brought a couple of her belongings, as you asked," Cheryl said, dipping into the bag she had brought. She gave the clairvoyant the diary and also a cashmere cardigan with wide sleeves, fashionably longer in the front than the back, which she explained Lydia had lent her.

"*Parfait*," Madame Mathilde said with satisfaction, taking the items.

"Would you like some wine?" Helen offered.

The Frenchwoman declined and requested herbal tea instead, which Helen went off to prepare while her guest wandered about the downstairs, seeking a suitable room for the séance. She selected the little-used dining room. "This will do very well," she announced. She crossed to the buffet and took one of a pair of candelabras and placed it in the center of the table.

Rex lit the white candles with a lighter kept in the top buffet drawer. "Should I switch off the lights?" he enquired.

Madame Mathilde acquiesced with a nod of her chin.

"Ehm, how does this work exactly?" he asked. "And what are we required to do?"

"We link hands and focus on the dearly departed with welcoming thoughts in an effort to summon her into our circle."

"And then what?" Cheryl asked, eyes green and round with fear in her elfin face.

"That depends. With the visions comes a feeling, sometimes calming, sometimes apprehensive, and at times frightening, especially when a violent death is concerned. Often the victims speak to me, but not with speech, precisely. It is usually more of an emotional communication." The psychic took in the attentive faces of her audience seated around the table and sipped the tea Helen had brought her. "Commissariats in Paris have utilised my services on occasion. *Eh, oui.* I once helped them locate the body of a young American student drowned in the Seine by the Pont Neuf. I described the bridge to the police and how he had taken a dose of sleeping pills and drunk a bottle of wine on the bank before slipping into the water. As well, I saw a vague, dreamlike image of a broken heart. And, sure enough, on his person was a *billet doux* written in his hand to a French girl who had spurned his proposal of marriage. *C'était très triste.*" Madame Mathilde shook her head sadly and wrapped her shawl tighter around her although it was not cold in the room.

"It must be hard for you to get involved," Helen said.

"But it is my calling, my vocation, and I feel I must use my gift to bring peace to the ones left behind."

"Certainly," Rex acknowledged, eager to proceed. He had waited a week to discover more about the deceased Gladstone couple. He waited a few more minutes while the psychic finished her herbal tea and told them how charming Lydia had been when they met on the plane. They had found themselves sitting next to each other in a row of three seats. Tom had been dosing during the short trip across northern France and the Channel, and Lydia had engaged her fellow passenger in conversation. When she found out the Frenchwoman's profession, she launched into her grief over the loss of her father and how she had heard his voice in her dreams. She asked Madame Mathilde if there was a way to reach him in the other world. Unfortunately, the psychic concluded with a desolate shrug, that séance had not come to pass due to Lydia's untimely demise.

"But, of course, she and her father are together now, and that is a consolation," she added.

"Did you foresee Lydia's death?" Helen enquired.

"I had a sense of foreboding," Madame Mathilde replied. "But I always feel that when I fly."

Rex refrained from smiling and looking at Helen to see her reaction. He cleared his throat. "If we're ready, shall we commence?" he asked the three women seated at the table.

~TEN~

With apparent concentration, Madame Mathilde fondled the cream cashmere cardigan that had belonged to Lydia and ran gentle fingers through the pages of her diary. She placed the journal on the table in front of her and let the garment slip to her lap. She held out a hand to the women either side of her and bid everyone let their minds go blank so they might alter their awareness and be open to the spirit they were hoping to summon. Easier said than done, Rex thought, clasping Helen's left hand and Cheryl's right. Miming the psychic, the young woman bowed her head and closed her eyes tight. Rex tried to think of grey nothingness, as he did when trying to get to sleep and rid his mind of obtrusive, reoccurring thoughts after a long and fraught workday. He could hear everyone's breathing and tried to regulate his.

"Do you have a message for your friend, *Shereel?*" Madame Mathilde asked at last. "Speak up, my child."

"I miss you, Lydia!" Cheryl blurted. "I need to know what happened. I want to help!" She started sobbing.

"It is no use," Madame Mathilde said after a while. "I cannot get a connection." She glanced at Rex with pinched lips as though he were somehow at fault.

Cheryl's narrow shoulders slumped.

"Would it help if I were to leave the room?" Rex asked. "Perhaps Lydia's spirit is not receptive to me?"

"It is not that," the psychic replied. "It is the atmosphere. Somewhere more familiar might be better. Was Lydia ever at this house?" she asked Helen.

"She only ever came to the front door, that I remember. When we went jogging."

"I'm afraid I cannot summon her, perhaps because she is a new spirit. She is being reticent, I think."

"What if we go over to her house?" Cheryl suggested. "I have a key. The electricity is still on."

Madame Mathilde nodded approval. "But I believe the spirits prefer candles."

"We can take these candles. Anyway, Lydia has some in her house. She has loads around her bath."

Rex coughed to interrupt them. "That's trespassing," he warned.

"She was my best friend! I want—need!—to find out what happened to her." Cheryl turned back to Madame Mathilde. "What do you say?"

"It would be more appropriate to try there," the psychic agreed. "Anyway, it is your fee, or rather, Mr. Graves', and I will comply with his wishes."

Cheryl gazed in appeal at Rex. He glanced at Helen who shrugged. "Aye, all right, but the police would not look kindly on our holding a séance at a crime scene."

"It's been weeks. Anyway, they won't find out unless a neighbour reports us," Cheryl said. "I'm sure Lydia's mum wouldn't mind. And Tom's parents are back home in Berkshire."

"Then let us go," Madame Mathilde directed, rising from the table.

Helen went to turn the ceiling light back on. Rex blew out the candles, leaving tendrils of smoke. The psychic retrieved the red bag and put Lydia's diary and cardigan in it. Helen added the candelabra and lighter. When they had all donned coats and jackets, they trooped outside, deciding it would draw less attention if they walked. The Gladstone house wasn't far.

The air felt sharp with cold and the stars shone stark and bright. The homes they passed were mothballed in silence, with only an occasional window faintly lit behind a curtain. No dog barked and no cars entered the cul-de-sac. As they made their way, with Rex and the psychic leading the small group, Madame Mathilde asked him details about the Gladstone case.

"I only know what I read in the papers," she explained. "I recognized their photos immediately. They were an attractive couple. Who would have wanted to harm them, if that is what happened? And by using antifreeze… It is very strange. I hope Lydia will be able to reveal something."

"As do I. But antifreeze poisoning is not so very uncommon," Rex said, speaking from professional experience, having prosecuted two murder cases where radiator coolant had been used.

Upon approaching the Gladstone house, everyone grew quiet. He now regretted agreeing to Cheryl's bringing in Madame Mathilde for a séance. He had no truck with psychics, mediums, mentalists, or however else they referred to themselves. He gave Helen a significant look over his shoulder.

Cheryl caught it. "It'll be fine," she assured him. "Lydia would want this. She'd want the person who did this to her and Tom to be brought to justice."

Rex was growing doubtful they would find out anything useful and thought how embarrassing it would be if they were caught in the victims' house, which was still swathed in sagging police tape. However, Cheryl had already been inside rummaging for the diary, which she had essentially stolen from the property, whether it had been Lydia's wish for her friend to retrieve it or not. Cheryl drew a bunch of keys from her pocket and slid one into the front door lock. Rex looked about the street. There was no one in view. They all four slipped into the dark hallway, and Cheryl closed the door softly behind them. The chill air seemed unnaturally still, as though waiting with suspended breath. Helen took Rex's hand, and he squeezed it reassuringly. Yet even he felt the presence of death in the house in a way that made the hairs on the back of his neck stand on end.

"Brrr, it is cold," Madame Mathilde murmured, the first to speak. "The heating must be off."

Cheryl switched on the torch she had brought from her car and flashed its beam down the wide marble-tiled hallway. "We can use Tom's study at the back of the house. It's the most private room downstairs and has an electric fire."

When they were gathered in the study she drew the heavy curtains across the windows overlooking the back garden and lit the four candles in the candelabra, which she placed on a card table by the window. The surrounding furniture and ornaments jumped into relief in the glow of the tapering flames. The logs in the fireplace, when switched on, burned a warm amber and gave off a comforting heat.

"*Merci, Shereel,*" Madame Mathilde said, though nobody removed their outer layers of clothing. It was as though no one wanted to make themselves appear too much at home in this sinister house.

~ELEVEN~

Tom's study was a quintessentially masculine room furnished at one end with a heavy desk and a burgundy leather executive chair missing its padded seat, which Rex guessed had been removed by the crime scene investigators. He recalled with discomfort that Tom's body had been found slumped in that chair. On closer inspection, he could make out the powdery residue of fingerprint dust on its back and arms, and likewise on the desk. He warned the others not to touch either item of furniture and as little as possible of the rest of the room.

A photo of Tom with Lydia and his two children posing on a picnic blanket sat on the desk. Hannah was an adorable blonde pre-schooler, her older half-brother a shyly smiling boy who more resembled Daniel than Tom, in Rex's opinion.

Standing in the deceased's study made him feel even more of an intruder. The light from the fireplace and candles illuminated a collection of framed certificates and awards on the walls and a bag of golf clubs in a shadowy corner by the door. Rex crossed to the tall bookcase to gain a better sense of Tom Gladstone and, peering at the spines, saw titles mainly related to business and history, interspersed with biographies of world leaders. On one shelf stood an assortment of liqueur bottles on a silver tray, along with a stainless steel ice bucket equipped with tongs.

"*Ah, tenez, une bouteille d'Absinthe*," Madame Mathilde noted at his side. "In the past, Absinthe was referred to as '*la fée verte*,' the green fairy, owing to its colour and reputed psychoactive properties." She reached towards the bottle, which Tom and Lydia had brought back from Paris, before withdrawing her hand at Rex's instruction. "*Bon*," she announced, turning away from the bookshelf. "Shall we try again?"

Rex sensed rather than observed his companions' apprehension. They arranged themselves as before, with him seated opposite Madame Mathilde, and they prepared their minds as previously instructed.

"Lydia, come to us," the psychic intoned. "We come with good intentions. Manifest your presence, my child." Madame Mathilde fell into a trance-like state. Her face appeared transfigured, aglow in the light of the candles. Nothing happened for a while. Suddenly she gasped. Her manicured hands, released from her partners', fluttered above the table. Rex and Helen exchanged surreptitious glances. "Yes, I feel your presence now. You are among friends, do not be afraid. Speak to me, Lydia. Tell me what happened in this house!" She paused. "I sense a cold heart," she pursued. "And a fiery one. I see a redhead, a broken circle. A reconnection. And—" The psychic gave a sudden jolt in her chair, and her eyes flew open.

Rex who had been watching all this time through his eyelashes, rose from the table and groped for the light switch over by the door. "Whatever is the matter?" he asked the Frenchwoman seated still and silent as stone.

She drew a deep breath, as though she had been under water for too long. "At first I felt the usual *frisson*, alerting me to the presence of a spirit hovering in the room. I picked up on a dark energy. Then I saw the images of which I spoke. The visitation did not last long, but it was intense. There is evil in this house, of that I am sure."

Cheryl cringed in her chair. "Did you see Lydia?"

"Only the glimpse of a smile, cruel and hard." Madame Mathilde shivered, and then added, "Can't be sure whose it was. I am sorry."

"Should we try summoning Tom for answers?" Helen asked. "His possessions are all over the room."

The psychic remained mute, apparently reluctant to proceed.

"Aye, we've come this far." Rex, who had been secretly recording the audio on his phone, decided he had not yet received his penny's worth out of the séance.

Madame Mathilde nodded briefly. *"D'accord,"* she agreed with grim purpose.

Rex turned off the light. They linked hands again around the table. Cheryl gripped Rex's fingers, her eyes scrunched closed. She was obviously terrified. He pressed her hand in his and did the same with Helen's. This had better not be a hoax, he thought. Though generally a good judge of character, he found it hard to get a read on Madame Mathilde.

"Tom," the psychic called out, causing the three others to jump. "We have come for answers. There is something not right. I feel your spirits are restless and trapped. Am I correct?"

The golf bag in the corner of the study toppled over with a dull thud and clatter of iron. Cheryl let out a cry. Everyone looked over to where the noise had emanated, except Madame Mathilde who was deep in a trance. "You are troubled, Tom. Yes, *mon ami*, I can feel your rage." This time a large tome slid backwards on the bookshelf landing heavily on the wood. Either there was a poltergeist in the room or they were experiencing an earthquake tremor. Rex could not decide which was more probable. Cheryl glanced at him in alarm, tightening her grip of his hand. He motioned with his mouth to keep quiet. He and the two women turned their attention back to the psychic. The candles went out suddenly and Rex could see only her silhouette backlit by the fire in the smoky silence.

"*Ce n'est pas possible!*" she declared, shaking herself out of her trance. She snatched her hands from those beside her and put the knuckles to her cheeks. "*C'est diabolique.*"

"What is not possible?" Helen asked in dismay while Rex went for the light switch. "What is diabolical?"

"We must leave at once," Madame Mathilde responded, scrambling to her feet.

"Are we in danger?" Cheryl tipped the card table as she sprang from her chair in a panic. Rex caught the candelabra before the candles could burn the green baize, but hot wax dripped onto it. The freckles stood out in the young woman's face. "It was murder, wasn't it?" she asked Madame Mathilde.

"Murder most violent," the psychic replied, holding the variegated green scarf to her throat. "But my visions were muddled. Let us go!"

Cheryl stuffed Lydia's cardigan and diary into

the bag and Rex turned off the electric fire. Silently, they left the house. As they proceeded down the street, Rex entreated the psychic for more details. All he had thus far was her report of a redhead, a circle, a cruel smile, an irate husband, and her conviction that intentional murder had been perpetrated at the residence. She declined to answer his entreaty, visibly shaken by the séance and tightening her black cloak around her.

Frustrated by her reticent attitude and suspecting her words to be a load of paranormal mumbo-jumbo, Rex asked Helen the colour of Tom's ex-wife's hair. Natalie had been the only known visitor to the house that fateful Sunday night.

"Red," Helen told him.

Now, how could the psychic have known that? He wondered.

~TWELVE~

When the four of them returned to Helen's house, Madame Mathilde cordially took her leave after accepting the envelope Rex handed to her containing her fee. She proffered her business card in case he knew of anyone who might benefit from her services and, still agitated by what she had experienced during the séances, got into her car and drove off without further delay.

"Fancy a nightcap?" Helen asked Cheryl.

"If you really don't mind. I feel too shaky to drive just yet, but I won't stay long. I have to work in the morning."

"What do you do?" Rex asked their guest when they were comfortably seated in the living room. He decided to keep off the subject of the séances for now in view of her frame of mind.

"Event planning for businesses," the young woman replied. "Lydia and I started the company together. Then she got offered the marketing position at Fruité Furniture and a share in the profits, since it was her brainchild. It was better paid, so I totally understood why she chose to do that."

"So you're on your own now?"

"I have an assistant, but it's not the same. First I lose my business partner and then my best friend," Cheryl lamented.

Helen offered a few words of sympathy while Rex went off to the kitchen to prepare coffee.

"So, what did you make of Madame Mathilde?" he asked Cheryl who seemed more composed when he returned to the sitting room. "Do you think she was having us on?"

"Oh, not at all. I'm sure it was real. Did you see how affected she was?"

Or else the French psychic was a consummate actress, he thought, stirring his coffee. However, some of the night's proceedings were not explained away so lightly. "She had her back to the golf clubs and bookcase," he mused aloud. "Unless she pulled magic strings, I don't see how she could have made those objects fall over. Or the candles go out."

"She could have blown them out while we weren't looking," Helen said.

"I was peeping the whole time. Something supernatural had to have been going on, or else some very clever trickery. But she was holding your and Cheryl's hand."

"It was spooky." Helen rubbed her upper arms. "I did feel something—like we weren't alone. As though someone unseen were in the room."

"Perhaps there was."

"So much for bringing messages of comfort from the dead," Cheryl said from one end of the sofa, where her tiny frame was ensconced in a pile of cushions. "That's what I thought spiritualists did. I was hoping Lydia would communicate with me. And yet something Madame Mathilde said struck a chord."

"What was that?" Rex asked, leaning forward in his armchair.

"When she saw someone's smile. Lydia did have a certain smile, not cruel, exactly, but full of...how can I put it?"

"Malice?" Helen suggested. "Or is that overstating it?"

"Maybe wicked would be more accurate. But in a playful sort of way. It was when she got one up on someone... Like the time she overheard a young intern talking in the break room about how Tom had French-kissed her under the mistletoe at the Christmas party when no one was looking. Lydia told me she went out to the parking lot right then and there and keyed her car. I was a bit shocked that she would react that way; you know, wilfully causing damage to someone's property, but she was provoked, she said. Still, it was more

Tom's fault than the intern's."

"I hope the kiss was worth it," Helen remarked with cynicism. "But I agree: Tom shouldn't have been abusing his power with an intern half his age."

Rex thought the incident gave an interesting insight into both Lydia and her husband's characters. "Do you know who the intern is?" he asked Cheryl.

"I don't even know her name. But I think Lydia said she left the firm."

"And what do you make of that other vision of Madame Mathilde's, to do with a redhead?" he enquired. "Do you lend any credence to Natalie being involved in the murders?"

Cheryl shook her blond curls, and then shrugged, as though revising her opinion. "It's possible, I suppose. She was there, after all. She might have seized the opportunity and put antifreeze in their drinks. I'd spoken to Lydia on the phone earlier that evening. I remember her speech was slurred, and it sounded like she dropped the phone. I thought she might be drinking more than usual. I heard Tom say something in the background and Lydia telling him to shut up."

Rex recalled slurring of speech was a symptom of antifreeze poisoning. "Are you sure it was Tom?"

"I'm sure of it. It sounded like he was making a joke. He has—had—a quite distinctive voice, sort of plummy."

"Plummy?"

"Deep and resonant," Helen assisted Cheryl, who was frowning as though concentrating to find the right words to describe it. "Like a radio announcer's voice. Is that what you mean, Cheryl?"

The young woman nodded. "It would be hard to mistake."

"Did you hear anything after that?" Rex asked.

"No. I said, 'Lydia? Lydia?' but the phone went dead."

"Would you describe her as an habitual drinker?"

Cheryl considered the question. "A moderate drinker. She got tipsy and giggly when she drank, but I never saw her intoxicated to the point of being out of control."

Rex reflected for a moment. "Natalie might have joined Lydia and Tom for a drink while the children were asleep on the sofa and administered the antifreeze. What did they usually have?"

"Lydia liked white wine. Tom sometimes had whisky."

"The antifreeze I've seen is fluorescent green, which would have been a bit obvious if mixed with white wine. Ethylene glycol, the main component of antifreeze, takes a while to have an effect.

Perhaps Natalie arrived earlier than she stated to police and did not find them dead like she said."

"Lydia and I spoke on the phone at around six," Cheryl told him. "They had just arrived back from their family day out. Lydia would've mentioned if Natalie was there. She said she was due to arrive at eight to collect Devin."

"Amazing the bairns slept through the whole thing."

"Lydia told me they'd taken Hannah and Devin to visit Chatsworth House, you know, where they filmed *Pride and Prejudice*, and the kids were worn out."

"I'm not surprised," Rex remarked. The stately home was palatial and the grounds stretched across acres. He and Helen had spent an afternoon there last May. The rhododendrons by the formal lake had been gorgeous, the grey stone balustrades and sweeping terraces an ideal setting for a Regency romance.

"And Tom, who was feeling under the weather, had to sit some of it out," Cheryl continued. "Lydia said she drove them home. But the parents all got on really well. I don't see why Natalie would have wanted Tom and Lydia dead."

"Perhaps she wanted sole custody of Devin." Helen, who had been listening to the conversation without interrupting until that point, stretched back on the sofa and yawned.

Cheryl shook her head in the negative. "I think it suited her to have Devin spend alternate weekends with his dad. It gave her and Matt a chance to take off for short breaks."

Rex recalled Natalie's second husband was a dentist. Was it time for a check-up? he wondered. If Natalie wouldn't speak to Helen, perhaps he could speak to Dr. Purvis. His hand automatically reached for his jaw, where he'd had a filling replaced a year ago. He could still hear the whine of the drill. The dentist's chair would not be his first choice of venue to conduct an informal interview, but needs must.

"Why are you looking so pained?" Helen asked with concern.

"I was thinking of paying Dr. Purvis a visit and seeing if he could throw light on the subject under discussion. I'm due for a cleaning."

"Is that so?" Helen said with an amused smile. "However, you may be spared the ordeal. Jill went yesterday. She's coming over in the morning to fill us in."

"That's the sort of *filling* I like," Rex joked. "I'm relieved I won't have to personally resort to drastic measures to *extract* information."

"Very funny. But I haven't spoken to Jill yet, so I don't know what she was able to find out. She said she gets on well with him, so I doubt he'd mind her showing some friendly interest in the case."

"So, Jill is on this case too?" Cheryl asked in surprise.

"It sort of snowballed," Rex explained.

"Why don't you stay over," Helen invited, "instead of driving home tonight, and have Sunday brunch with the three of us? I can make up the bed in the spare room."

"That's really kind, but Tabs will be waiting for me. That's Hannah's cat I adopted. And I really do have to work tomorrow. We're preparing for a national acupuncturists' convention on Monday at the Clover Hotel. It's quite a big do. I'm sorry I suggested the séance now. I hope you make more headway with Jill than with Madame Mathilde."

"I'm only sorry it distressed you, lass. Time may yet tell if the fragmented images make any sense. Perhaps you could go through the diary again and see if anything pops out after this evening's developments?" Not that there had been much in the way of developments beyond a couple of moving objects, Rex recalled. "Or, if you prefer, perhaps you'd care to entrust me with reading it. You know…an objective pair of eyes?"

Cheryl shook her blond curls and pursed her mouth. "It's not that I don't trust you," she said. "And you've been very good to me, retaining Madame Mathilde's services, and everything. But I just don't think Lydia would have wanted a stranger reading her journal. I will go through it again," she promised, "and let you know of anything." She got up and hugged him and Helen goodbye.

"Rex, dear, I hope the coffee isn't going to keep you awake," Helen said when Cheryl had left.

"If it doesn't, my thoughts probably will."

"I'm sure I'll have nightmares. I don't think I've ever witnessed anything as bizarre as what happened in Tom's study. I didn't want to say so in front of Cheryl, but now I think I might actually believe in ghosts and evil spirits."

"Aye, it was an experience, all right, and not one I'd like repeated," Rex agreed most wholeheartedly. Talk about things that go bump in the night.

~THIRTEEN~

Rex's thoughts kept him wakeful for an hour that night. Madame Mathilde's visions had given him food for thought. And would Cheryl find anything of significance in her second reading of the journal? Would Jill's visit to the dentist have yielded new information?

When Helen's neighbour arrived promptly at ten-thirty the next morning bearing a prickly cactus in a small, hand-painted earthenware pot, the kitchen table was set for breakfast and the food and coffee ready to be served.

Helen thanked Jill for the gift and placed it on the window sill. "There," she said with a pleased smile. "It certainly cheers up the view on this dreary morning." She turned to her friend. "So how did you get on at the dentist?"

Jill bared her teeth. "Whiter, smoother, and no cavities to report."

"And...," Helen prompted, serving the eggs, bacon, black pudding, and tomato on the three plates lined up on the counter.

"And," Jill said, "I did get some information out of Dr. Purvis. As much as I could, anyway, with a saliva tube stuck in my mouth. He's quite gabby, fortunately," she addressed Rex, "and once he got talking he didn't stop even with his mask on. So I just lay back in the dentist's chair and made sympathetic and encouraging noises."

Rex brought the rack of toast to the table and poured out the coffee. "Rather you than me. I was going to make an appointment to see him myself."

Jill laughed. "You'd actually go to such lengths?"

"We didn't have any luck with Natalie," Helen said, distributing the plates on the table and sitting down opposite her friend. "She was reluctant to talk to me."

"Well, I started by asking after her and, according to her husband, she's taking Tom's death really hard. Finding him dead in his study and then Lydia unconscious upstairs has haunted her. She's on sedatives, apparently. They took a trip to Portugal, which helped a little, but Dr. Purvis said she's still very nervy, and Devin is moping about the house. They told him his dad died from food poisoning, because they don't think he's old enough to fully understand the concept of murder, which Dr. Purvis is convinced is what happened. He said one accidental death was believable; two was suspicious."

"Unless one of the children gave Tom and Lydia antifreeze thinking it was juice." Helen said, putting forward Daniel Gladstone's theory. She passed Jill the butter dish.

"I don't think Devin would confuse a container of antifreeze with juice," Jill countered. "Not saying he couldn't have stood on something and reached up to get it, but I think he'd have known better than to give it to someone to drink. Tom was quite strict with his kids from what I saw. Perhaps more so with Devin. Hannah was definitely a daddy's girl. You could see how proud he was of her. Anyway, it's a tragic business, whichever way you look at it. But Dr. Purvis didn't or wouldn't elaborate on his suspicions."

Rex smiled at Jill. "Still, it sounds like you managed to learn quite a bit under your constrained circumstances."

"Like I said, he's is a jolly sort of chap, good at putting people at their ease. A couple of casual questions from me and away he went. And perhaps he's not overly concerned his wife's ex is out of the picture."

"I only met him once," Helen remarked. "I thought he was a nice man and quite attractive, though not as striking as Tom."

"Given the choice, I'd take Matt Purvis over Tom for a husband any day of the week," claimed the single Jill. "A much safer bet. But I'd have a fling with Tom first," she added with a grin.

"Ladies, ladies," Rex admonished in jest, shaking his head.

The three of them concentrated on their breakfast for a few moments, until Jill exclaimed, "Oh, I almost forgot about your séance last night. How did that go?"

Rex and Helen glanced at each other. "Unnerving," Helen blurted at the same time as Rex said, "strange."

Jill dabbed at her mouth with the blue linen napkin. "Well?" she prodded.

Rex let Helen describe the events of the previous evening, which she did matter-of-factly, though her voice revealed a tremor when it came to Tom's part in the proceedings. Jill listened with her mouth open in disbelief.

"It must have been a set-up," she said when Helen had finished her account. "There wasn't thunder last night, was there?" she asked, puzzled. "Nothing that could have shaken the house and caused the golf bag and book to topple over?"

"It wasn't just that," Helen told her. "I actually felt goose bumps. And then the candles went out all at once."

Jill continued to look doubtful. "Coming from anyone but you, Helen, I wouldn't believe it. But, remember, it's a draughty old house. Or could this

Madame Mathilde be a fraud?"

"She seemed genuine enough," Helen replied. "I scoured the Internet this morning. Mostly glowing testimonials and debts of gratitude from people she had put in touch with their dearly departed. And it seems she has a good reputation with the Paris police, who go to her for assistance on occasion."

"The episode last night appeared to unsettle her," Rex added. "I think she may have seen more than she let on."

"Why wouldn't she reveal everything?" Jill asked with scepticism.

"She seemed confused by what she had witnessed. It's as though she were caught off guard."

"Hm," was all Jill said in response to his explanation.

"There was a lot of turbulence in that house last night," Helen insisted as she got up from the table to clear the large plates. "Madame Mathilde mumbled something about restless spirits being trapped within the walls. And that vision of the redhead... Natalie had the means and opportunity to poison her ex-husband and Lydia."

"I don't know," Jill said carefully. "One other thing Dr. Purvis said, now that I think about it, was that upon finding the bodies, his wife immediately called nine-nine-nine and then him.

He arrived seconds before the police and got the kids out of the house before they realized what had happened. Devin was very excited when he saw the emergency vehicles and asked a lot of questions, as eight year-olds do. The police questioned him, but he hadn't seen or been aware of anything unusual. They'd had pizza and tutti-frutti ice cream when they got back from Chatsworth, he said, and then he and Hannah had a bath and watched a Harry Potter film while waiting for his mum to collect him. He'd fallen asleep before the end, and so had Hannah."

"Just as well," Helen remarked with a sad sigh, sitting back down at table. "But if it wasn't Natalie, who else could have arrived beforehand and poisoned the parents?"

"Unfortunately, no one in the cul-de-sac was paying attention to cars passing by," Jill said pensively. "People close their curtains early this time of year, and we don't have a resident nosy neighbour that I'm aware of. So the nanny, Uncle Rob, Daniel, Lydia's mum, or just about anybody could have visited Tom and Lydia, and since they were often at the house, it would be natural to find their fingerprints there."

"Daniel told me everyone closest to Tom and Lydia had solid alibis," Rex countered, "which, presumably, the detectives on the case verified. Still, alibis have been known to have holes in them, and people lie to the police all the time to protect those they love or feel threatened by. Is Uncle Rob married?"

"I think he was," Helen replied. "He still wears a wedding ring. I believe he's widowed."

Jill nodded. "For many years now. Don't know the details."

"He didn't feature in Madame Mathilde's visions," Helen said.

"Indeed." Rex buttered a second helping of toast. "And why murder his mistress and nephew who, by all accounts, were assets to his firm? Plus, it seems the family already knew about his affair with Lydia, so killing her off to silence her makes no sense." He shook his head in puzzlement. "Cheryl never explained why she suspects him. I'll have to ask her."

Helen served the three of them more coffee. "Perhaps she doesn't like him. I always thought he was a bit smarmy, myself."

"Smarmy?" Rex asked, amused.

"He wears quite a bit of jewellery," Jill said. "And a fake tan."

"Are we getting anywhere?" Helen asked Rex in mild frustration.

"Maybe. I'm going to seek out my next witness."

"And who might that be?"

"Young Tracy." She had been on his list since

the previous weekend, but he'd not had time to locate her.

Both women nodded in approval. "I saw an ad in the local paper," Jill informed him. "A trained nanny called Tracy is looking for babysitting jobs. I'm sure it's her."

"Thank you," Rex said. "I'll contact her on that number."

"I wonder if she'll have any luck finding a new position until the case is solved," Jill added. "If I were a parent I'd be hesitant to employ her."

"I know you and Helen regard Tracy as a prime suspect because you think she may have set her sights on Tom…"

"And because she probably knew about Lydia's affair with Rob and saw her chance. Plus she was at the house a lot."

"Was Tom having an affair with her, though? According to Lydia's diary, he had someone on the side, someone who wore expensive perfume, but was it Tracy?" While Rex acknowledged Jill's logic, it seemed everyone had a different and potentially plausible theory. Which one would prove correct was what he needed to find out while he still had the time to dedicate to this perplexing case.

~FOURTEEN~

After brunch, Rex sought out Tracy's number in the local paper and gave her a call. When he explained he was interested in speaking to her about the case, she said with obvious reluctance she would be at the park watching over two of her neighbour's boys if he wanted to meet her there. Seizing the opportunity, he left Helen and Jill talking in the kitchen and, taking his fiancée's car, followed the directions Tracy had given him to where she lived. It took twenty minutes to get there, during which time he considered what he was going to say.

The most alluring aspect of Cedar Grove, a new development of identical modest homes, was its centrally located park and children's playground, where he found whom he assumed to be Tracy supervising her charges as they wheeled around on a hexagonal metal roundabout. Adjacent stood a row of swings, and off to the side a see-saw and climbing frame, all in primary colours and occupied by a dozen rowdy pre-teens.

A couple of women sat chatting on a bench by the railings, while a man tossed a rubber ball to a spotted dog of indeterminate breed. Amid the barks, chatter, and squeals and shrieks from the playground, Rex approached the young blonde wrapped in a camel duffle coat and gave her his card, which she studied with a furrowed brow. She had sounded nervous on the phone, perhaps unable to summon up the courage to refuse him a meeting. Now it appeared she regretted her indecision and was thinking of a way to rebuff him.

"I really can't tell you anything," she blurted. "I'm sorry you came all this way."

"Well, I'm here now," he replied pleasantly.

"I spoke to my mum and she said I shouldn't say anything because there's a police investigation going on."

"She's right," Rex conceded. "Have you retained counsel?"

"A lawyer? What for? I'm not guilty of anything." Her pretty face pouted in defiance.

"Then you have nothing to hide. Perhaps we can talk on the bench?" He indicated one out of earshot of anyone else, yet close enough to the roundabout for her to keep an eye on the brothers. They wore matching rugby shirts and sported sticking plasters on their scuffed knees. A third boy grabbed the hand rail and spun them faster, running alongside in the muddy grass and then pushing away.

Tracy huddled down on the bench, hands deep in her pockets. Her fine platinum hair blew back in the breeze, her cheeks glowed pink from the bracing air. It was hard to gauge her figure in the heavy coat, but she appeared more fulsome than the diminutive Cheryl, and her periwinkle blue eyes were not as innocent, in spite of her younger age. Had Tracy been in love with Tom? Rex looked around at the rows of rectangular houses, where she presumably still lived with her parents, and further wondered if she had seen Tom as an attractive way out of a humdrum existence.

"I'm not with the Derby police or anything like that," he restated. "As I explained on the phone, my fiancée knew your employers, and since I sometimes work on private cases, I thought I'd look into this one."

"Have you spoken to Mrs. Simmons?"

"Who is Mrs. Simmons?"

"Lydia's mum," Tracy said in a mildly exasperated tone.

Good, thought Rex; she's beginning to think I'm a harmless old fool. "I spoke to Daniel Gladstone in person and have his support. Naturally, he wants to know how his brother and sister-in-law were poisoned."

"Why not let the detectives get on with their

jobs?" Tracy retorted, gaining assurance.

"I'm sure they are. I don't suppose they questioned you," he remarked, knowing full well they would have.

"Well, of course they did." Tracy glanced at him with an expression close to distain. "I was their nanny! I was with them for over a year." She straightened her shoulders in self-importance.

"Well, that makes you a valuable witness. I was under the impression you were just the babysitter," he said, feeling justified in lying in this one instance in view of her less than cordial attitude towards him. He began to think the only reason she had agreed to meet with him was because she didn't want to arouse suspicion by refusing. Now that she'd formed the opinion he didn't know anything, she began to relax and act superior.

"I'm only babysitting until I find full-time work," she said with a haughty sniff.

"And, unfortunately, your past employers can't furnish you with a reference," he said sympathetically, doubting Lydia would have given her a good one if she suspected her of stealing her valuables, or her husband.

When Tracy declined to comment, he asked, "Do you still see Hannah?"

She shook her head and then shrugged. "Mrs. Simmons is taking care of her granddaughter now. Don't know how she's managing," she added.

"Hannah is at that age where she's hard to reason with. I mean, she's a lovely child and everything, but she can be demanding."

"Precocious?" Rex recalled Jill referring to Hannah as Daddy's little girl. Had Tracy been jealous?

"Tom—that's Mr. Gladstone, but they insisted I called them Tom and Lydia—he spoilt her rotten. She'd wheedle and throw tantrums if she didn't get her own way."

Tracy's voice betrayed her working-class Derbyshire roots. Her delicate looks and careful demeanour were curiously at odds with her dialect, self-consciously toned down as it was. She didn't wear much make-up or a surfeit of trinkets like so many girls of her age. Her coat, suede boots, and what he could see of her jeans, were of good quality and in discreet taste. Here was a girl, he thought, desperate to rise out of her background, and a man like Tom could be her one-way ticket out.

"Derek!" she suddenly hollered at the boy on the roundabout leaning out with arms akimbo, one knee hooked around the rail preventing him from falling off. "Get back on properly or I'll take you both home," she threatened. He complied at leisure and then leapt off the platform and rushed towards the climbing frame, his two companions running after him and yelling with glee. "They're a right pair," she grumbled. "I much prefer girls."

"I have a grown son. Lads can be boisterous, I'll give you that."

"Devin's all right. Not like them two, anyway. Tom was stricter with him. The senior Mr. Gladstone is a strict man and probably treated Tom that way growing up."

Rex rather thought she liked saying her ex-employer's name. An incoming call on her phone interrupted the conversation. Rex leant back on the bench while she made arrangements for a babysitting job in the week. Another call followed on its heels, this time from a beau, whom she agreed to meet that evening, though not with any great enthusiasm. The indistinct male voice Rex heard did not belong to a mature man of the world; hence, perhaps, her laconic tone.

Had Tom Gladstone been drawn to much younger women? There had been that incident at the Christmas party with the intern, as relayed by Cheryl, but perhaps he just liked to flirt with them to prove he still had what it took. Rex remembered his packet of humbugs and drew it from his pocket. He offered Tracy one as she returned her phone to her coat, and was surprised when she accepted. They sucked and chewed in companionable silence for a few moments watching the trio tackling the climbing frame. Derek and his younger brother swung from the bars, imitating chimpanzees at the zoo with ooh-ooh-ooh noises and scratching gestures. Tracy gazed at them sullenly.

"I should give them bananas for lunch," she remarked around the sweet in her mouth.

"How long do you have them?"

"Until four, more's the pity."

He noticed she did not smile a lot. In fact, not once in his presence. Was she really shy, as Helen and Jill had described her, or was she simply not forthcoming? She was something of a paradox, and it seemed a lot went on behind those watchful, and perhaps calculating, blue eyes. What could he ask her without putting her on her guard?

"How about Lydia? Was she a good mum?" he ventured.

"She was okay. I suppose it's hard juggling a child and a career, but I was there five days a week and sometimes in the evening to help out. Mrs. Simmons came to babysit when I couldn't, and looked after Hannah while her parents were in Paris. The Gladstones didn't spend many evenings in, and once Hannah was in bed, they often went out."

"But they treated you well?"

"Couldn't complain." This was said in a tone that suggested she would if given half a chance. Rex decided to give her that chance.

"Being with a young child on your own, day in,

day out, is hard. Many people don't realize unless they've been there."

Tracy nodded vigorously. "Sometimes I wanted to tear my hair out, but they still had the energy after a day at the office to dress up and go out for dinner or to a party."

"I hear Lydia Gladstone was very glamorous," Rex said, interested to see her reaction.

"She could afford to be. She had some amazing jewellery and clothes."

Some of which jewellery had gone missing.

"Plus her mom owns a beauty parlour. Some women have all the luck."

"Tom cut quite a figure too. I saw a photo of him at his sister's wedding."

Tracy nodded, almost imperceptibly. Her cheek coloured over and above the pink hue from the cold. She turned her face away. Was that a tear trickling from the outer corner of her eye, or was it watering from the sting of a sharp gust of wind? Rex directed his gaze straight ahead and gave her time to recover.

"I should get the lads in before they catch their death of cold," she said with renewed composure, lifting her shoulder and brushing her wet cheekbone against the coat.

"I need to get going too. You have my card. Call me if you remember anything that might help in the case." As she got up from the bench, he stood also. "I don't suppose you have any idea what happened to your ex-employers?" he asked in a final gambit.

"I don't," she said, looking up at him. "I left their house at six on Friday when Lydia came home, and didn't hear what had happened to them until my mom woke me late that Sunday night to tell me I didn't need to go to work the next day. She'd seen on the news they were dead."

Tracy spun away and hurried in the direction of the climbing frame. He watched her with a measure of pity. He was certain her dreams had been dashed, but whether by her own doing he could not be sure.

~FIFTEEN~

His mind was still on his meeting with Tracy ten minutes later when he spotted a dumpy man in a crumpled suit unloading a vacuum cleaner from the boot of an old Rover. The car had lost its shine over the course of the years and was of a matt oxblood hue. Rex turned into the residential street of terraced homes and parked behind the vehicle. The man greeted Rex as he got out of his car and asked if he was interested in a bargain.

"You sound like you're from my neck of the woods," Rex said pleasantly.

"Dunfermline, originally," the salesman replied, setting the Hoover, an upright with a coiled suction tube, on the pavement. He stuck out his right hand. "Larry Leath."

"Ah, from Fife, across the water from me." Rex shook his hand and introduced himself. "I believe you were in my fiancée's neighbourhood; a month back, was it? Barley Close. Her friend bought one of your vacuum cleaners."

The man pushed his glasses up his nose. "Barley Close," he repeated pensively, pulling on his scruffy, yellowish grey beard. "Oh, aye. That's just down the road. Only made the one sale that morning, to a lady driving instructor. Some of the residents were a bit snooty. Not her, but them living in the larger homes. There was this one lass, a wee blonde wi' a bairn of aboot three. The woman was not much more than a bairn herself, but someone was taking care of her. Nice hoose, and huge sapphires in her ears and a diamond rock on her ring finger. Right fancy for day wear! I used to be in the jewellery business, so I know a real gem from a fake. Anyhoo, she said she didn't do business with travelling salesmen." Leath shook his head in disbelief. "I said I like to get oot and meet my customers. She said she had no need of a Hoover that had fallen off the back of a lorry, the cheek! And that she had a new, top-o'-the-line model. Then she slammed the door in my face!"

Rex deduced he was talking about Tracy, since there were no other children of Hannah's age on Helen's street. "A green door with a brass knocker?" Rex asked when the flushed man finally paused for breath.

"Aye. The hoose at the top of the cul-de-sac."

"She was the nanny."

"Noo!" The man looked stunned. "She said she was the lady of the hoose when I asked."

Wishful thinking on her part, thought Rex. "That was where a married couple overdosed on antifreeze."

The salesman again showed his surprise, his glasses riding up his nose to meet his unruly eyebrows. "The woman I met wasna the same one as on the telly, and I never met the husband, so I didna put two and two together. Thought it must be a different home…," the man trailed off, shaking his head. "Mind you, I don't pay much attention to the news. They make a lot of the stuff up just to promote ratings. Epidemics blown oot of all proportion, jumbo jets vanishing into thin air—in this day and age! That hasna happened since the Bermuda Triangle hoax. And dinna get me started on—"

"You don't happen to recall what day you visited Barley Close, do you?" Rex interrupted him, having no wish to get the man started on any more conspiracy theories.

"It would have been a weekday. I'm at my repair shop most Saturdays and I never work on the Sabbath." As Leath shut the lid of the boot, Rex noticed a pile of boxes and a toolkit in the back seat. He memorised the number plate, just to be thorough, and made an excuse to leave before the man could ask why he was interested in his visit to Barley Close.

As he got in his car and drove away, he

wondered about the image the salesman had provided of Tracy playing dress-up with Lydia's jewellery and pretending to be Tom Gladstone's wife. It comported so well with the impression he had formed of her in the park.

By the time he returned to Helen's house, Jill had left to give a lesson to a pupil due to take his driving test in the coming week. He would have to wait to tell her about his encounter with her salesman. Helen was eager to hear what he had made of Tracy and whether he now shared her and Jill's opinion that she was the poisoner. Rex admitted to being of two minds.

"I agree she appears to have had feelings for Tom. She said his name in a much softer way than she spoke of Lydia or even Hannah." He sank into the sofa and said pensively, "She doesn't seem happy."

"She never struck me as particularly happy," Helen remarked, settling in beside him, a novel bookmarked halfway in her hand. "And now she's lost Tom and her job."

"I found her a wee bit snitty, to be honest."

Helen laughed. "Poor Rex. Perhaps she was just having a bad day. But the girl I remember was quiet and almost deferential. Perhaps that was her nanny persona. In any case, did you get the impression she was capable of doing her employers in?"

Rex combed his beard thoughtfully with his fingers. "If Tom had been the one to succumb to acute poisoning, I might be tempted to believe he was poisoned by accident, with Lydia the intended victim, but the systematic poisoning poses a problem. Someone premeditated his murder. At a pinch I can see Tracy killing Lydia on purpose, but not Tom."

"Because she cared for him?"

"So it appears."

"What if he rejected her?" Helen asked. "Wouldn't that be a powerful motive for an impressionable young woman?"

"Possibly." He still felt Tracy more capable of killing her perceived rival, especially if she felt Lydia might sack her over the theft of her valuables. That crime had not been solved, and Lydia might only have been waiting to find a suitable replacement for Tracy. Moreover, he personally thought the girl had an attitude, and her mooning over Tom had probably not gone unnoticed by Lydia. He heard the rustle of a page being turned beside him and decided to give his brain a break from the case by catching up on the Sunday papers while Helen read her book.

Discouraged by the news on all fronts, he asked Helen what she thought about getting away in April to his remote lodge in the Highlands, which they had visited only once since the

Christmas holidays. Just the two of them, he suggested. She said she thought it was a lovely idea. He set the *Guardian* on the carpet and held out his arm to her. She snuggled close, stretching her legs the length of the sofa.

They got around to discussing the possibility of acquiring a dog when they were married, one they could take to the lodge and leave with Rex's mother when they went abroad. For that reason it would have to be a smaller dog. They decided on a black Scottish Terrier, and Helen came up with the not so original name of Scottie for the proposed pet.

When she took up her book again, Rex closed his eyes and within minutes dozed off into a dreamless nap. Helen awoke him some time later with a cup of tea.

"If you sleep much longer, you might have difficulty tonight."

He stretched and yawned. "But such a nice way to spend a Sunday afternoon!" He took a gulp of tea.

"That looks like Lydia's mother's car," Helen exclaimed as she was drawing the curtains. "She drives a burgundy Mercedes."

"Paula Simmons?" Rex asked with alacrity.

"There's only one place she could be going…"

He jumped up from the sofa, fully awake. "Fancy a walk?"

~SIXTEEN~

They grabbed their coats and headed towards the Gladstone house on foot, only slowing down when they came to within a stone's throw of the driveway, which was blocked by an older-model Mercedes sedan that looked almost purple in the light of the street lamp. Its occupant had vacated it, and lights appeared in the upstairs windows of the house.

Rex stopped beyond the car and sniffed the air. "Smells like rain."

"You're right," Helen said, loitering beside him.

"Still, we've been lucky with the weather this weekend."

They drew out the conversation while they waited.

"Oh, let me knot up your scarf for you. There, that's better," Helen patted the lapels of his overcoat. "What's she doing in there?" she muttered under her breath. "If we stand about

110

much longer, we'll begin to look obvious."

Just then, the door burst open and a statuesque brunette in a padded sleeveless jacket exited the front door carrying a large cardboard box in her arms. Rex rushed up to the police tape and lifted it so she could pass under it.

"Hello, Mrs. Simmons," Helen called out brightly.

The woman, harried and breathless, acknowledged Helen with a brief nod. Rex introduced himself and offered to take the box to her car.

"Oh, would you?" The aging beauty wore her dark hair up in a lacquered bun, her black eyeliner applied in the Cleopatra look in vogue in the sixties. Retro primrose earrings in pink plastic studded her ears. "Thank you!" she gasped, handing him her burden. "Helen, isn't it?" she said, turning to his fiancée. "I so very much appreciated the condolence card you sent. It's been a terrible time and I haven't had a chance to reply to everyone yet," she hurried on in a marked Midlands accent.

"Absolutely no need, especially now we've run into each other," Helen assured her. "We were just taking a pre-dinner walk."

Mrs. Simmons held out her key fob and beeped open the boot of her Mercedes. She extracted an empty box and Rex placed the full one inside the car. "I came for the rest of Hannah's toys, poor child. I'm doing my best to take care of her on my own." She gave a sigh of woe.

"That can't be easy," Helen said.

"It isn't. None of it is. The solicitor is dragging his feet over Lydia's will, not that Lydia had much in the way of liquid assets. They were mortgaged up to the eyeballs on this house. But she and Tom each had life insurance policies. I was named as the contingent beneficiary in the one she took out on Tom, which is just as well since I now have Hannah to take care of, but that's been delayed as well."

"It's fortunate Lydia had the foresight to take precautions in the event the worst happened," Helen sympathised.

Paula Simmons nodded doubtfully. "I'm going back in to get some of my daughter's belongings, which I know she would have wanted me to have."

While Tom's parents were in Berkshire, Rex noted to himself.

"Her collection of Sade CDs and French recipe books," she added. "Just stuff of sentimental value."

Rex nodded in understanding, though he could not help but notice a jewellery case and silver figurines tucked in among the stuffed toys and children's books in the first box. "Can I be of further assistance?" he asked.

"You'd better not come in." Mrs. Simmons didn't know he had been inside the house the night before for the séance. "But if you could perhaps wait at the door and help me with the box when I come out?"

"Of course."

"I won't go in Tom's study or the upstairs bathroom." She shuddered before passing under the blue-and-white tape, which Rex lifted for her once again.

He walked with her up to the door while Helen stayed behind by the car. They waited patiently while Paula went in to load her second box. In the meantime, Rex mulled over what she had said about the life insurance policies. Presumably the insurance carrier wanted to know more about the circumstances of death before disbursing the funds to Lydia's estate. They might not pay out on suicide, especially if the policy was less than a year old. Since Paula Simmons was struggling financially even before she had care of Hannah, it could suit her from a practical standpoint to have Tom's death ruled accidental or malevolent so she could collect. Chances were she wasn't named anywhere in the policy he had held on Lydia. In the event she died as well, his immediate family would benefit.

It was growing colder as evening approached. While Helen walked back and forth along the pavement to keep warm, he stamped his feet on the bristled outdoor mat. He finally heard something heavy land on the other side of the door, and the downstairs lights went out shortly afterwards. The door opened and Mrs. Simmons appeared, her face flushed from exertion, her stiffly sprayed hair-do yet still in place. Rex reached inside the hall for the box and lifted it and its contents, which shifted about under the closed flaps.

"Sorry to keep you," she said, locking the front door. "I tried to be quick. My neighbour is minding Hannah for an hour. It really is so kind of you to help."

"Not at all. I never had the pleasure of meeting your daughter," he said as they returned to her car, "But Helen tells me she was a remarkable young woman, quite the wit and belle of the ball."

"My daughter did have a wicked sense of humour. She was very clever, and strong-willed. An only child. Her father, may he rest in peace, doted on her." Paula Simmons let out a deep sigh. "Lydia and Tom both had dominant personalities." Another woeful sigh. "I truly believe it's her behaviour that got her killed." She looked back at the house with a look more of curiosity than distress.

"How do you mean?" Rex asked. For a woman who had recently lost her only child, she seemed peculiarly in control of her emotions.

"Carrying on with Tom's uncle to get her own

back, for one thing," Paula Simmons replied. "Playing with fire, she was."

"Get her own back for what?" he asked, taken aback. Why would she talk about her dead daughter as though her death were her own fault, and even served her right? He placed the loaded box beside the other in the car.

"Tom was seeing his ex-wife, if you follow my drift. Yes," Paula Simmons said upon noting Rex's surprise, and Helen's. "They were cheating on their new spouses with each other. If you ask me, Tom couldn't bear to see Natalie married to someone else, someone with 'Doctor' before his name, even though he divorced her for Lydia. She followed him one afternoon, waited outside Natalie's house for almost an hour, and watched him leave, cocky as you please, with half his shirt buttons undone. Probably in a hurry to get away before the husband returned from his dental practice. I warned my daughter that tomcat might cheat on her. Tigers don't change their stripes, I told her. Or is it leopards changing their spots? Of course, she never listened. But cheating with his uncle... That was a slap in the face, and she knew it."

That's exactly what Daniel Gladstone had said, Rex recalled. "So who do you think was responsible for your daughter's death?" he asked.

"Who do you think?" With that, she gave Helen a brief hug, thanked Rex again for his help, and got in her Mercedes. The car rumbled to life, executed a laborious U-turn, and took off down the road.

"Imagine that!" Helen exclaimed watching the retreating taillights. "Tom and Natalie, and Lydia and Uncle Rob!"

"Keeping it in the family." Rex started walking. "We might never have known but for Paula divulging that wee bit of gossip... Do you think it's true?" But even as he asked, he remembered Cheryl telling him about Tom's extended absences when picking up and dropping off Devin. And why would Lydia's own mother make up such a thing—unless she was making excuses for her daughter's affair?

"I think in retrospect it might be true," Helen replied after a pause, linking his arm as they made their way back to her house. "Perhaps the chumminess wasn't so forced, after all. At least, not on Natalie and Tom's part."

"It must have been very hurtful for Lydia when she discovered the truth," Rex said. "By the sounds of it, our jolly Dr. Purvis remains in ignorant bliss, until Paula opens her mouth to *him*. Wonder what Tom really thought of her. Not sure I'd want her as a mother-in-law."

He thought hauling off the family silver when Tom's bereaved parents were in Berkshire was a bit underhand, though he had never met the elder

Mr. and Mrs. Gladstone and could not know what Paula's relations with them were like. Eluding him too was why Lydia had not mentioned Natalie by name when writing about Tom's affair. She would surely have recognized the expensive perfume she alluded to in her journal as belonging to the first wife. Women tended to be attuned to such details.

It seemed everyone involved held one tiny piece of the puzzle and, until all the pieces were put together, no clear picture could emerge.

~SEVENTEEN~

After dinner, Rex called Cheryl to ask if she knew about Tom's affair with his ex-wife, and she said she hadn't. She sounded shocked.

"When did you speak to Paula?" she enquired after he told her that Mrs. Simmons had revealed that information. "She's probably lying."

"Earlier this evening. Helen and I decided to take a walk when we saw her car in the cul-de-sac. We assumed she had business at Lydia's house."

"And?" Cheryl gasped over the phone.

"She had gone in to collect some items."

The young woman gave a short laugh. "She always was a scrounger, that one, crying poverty to Tom and Lydia and asking for money, which Tom would refuse and Lydia would pay behind his back. Paula's late husband didn't leave her much, and her salon is in trouble. She can't seem to keep her hairdressers and nail techs for long."

Obviously, Cheryl was no fan of Paula's. She added that Lydia hadn't mentioned Tom's affair with Natalie in her diary, just alluded to an anonymous affair. "It isn't an intimate diary, as I said before, except for her secret assignations with Tom's uncle. It's mostly factual, like what she did each day: Appointments, engagements, and such, though she records 'firsts' with Hannah, like her tying a ribbon, and all those endearing things, or not so endearing, like putting Tabs in the dryer. And she bitches on about Tracy, convinced the nanny steals her things and tries on her clothes when she's out of the house, and how she gets all moony in Tom's presence. Makes me wonder why she put up with her. Then there are pages about Paris when she got back. Presumably she didn't take her diary with her. It almost reads like a sightseeing guide, but for the romantic dinners and nights of *amour* at their ritzy hotel. Wait a sec while I get it…"

Rex listened to the soft thud of steps running up carpeted stairs at Cheryl's end. "Here's a typical entry dating back to mid-January," she resumed, sounding out of breath. "People are mostly referred to by their initials. It says, 'Hannah stayed in with a cold. T. has the symptoms again and is feeling run down. Had to phone N. to tell her it would be better not to risk Dev catching anything. She was pissed because she and Matt had already made plans. Met R. for lunch and a quickie at his place.' That would be Rob Gladstone," Cheryl explained as though Rex couldn't guess.

The thing that struck him most about the entries he'd heard were how unemotional they were. "By the way, why do you suspect Rob Gladstone?" he asked Cheryl. "That's what you told me when we first met."

"He's the only person in the family capable of murder. He's very driven. Daniel isn't ruthless. And I can't see someone outside the family, friend or colleague, doing it. I'm positive they were murdered. Lydia never mentioned any enemies at work. Even if she didn't tell me about Natalie—if that's true—she told me if she was having problems at the office. And we had the same circle of friends. I can't for the life of me think of one who would have wanted to kill her and Tom."

"And the poisoning wasn't a spur of the moment thing," Rex said. "At least, Tom's wasn't."

"Right. It had been going on for some time, if that's what his flu-like symptoms were. Lydia refers to his condition throughout. She says he was unable to shake his flu in early January and went to the doctor. Then he seemed to get better, and by the time they went to Paris he had recovered, and was still fine a week later at the party. And then the symptoms came back."

"Fatally this time," Rex said.

He thought it significant that Tom had been well in Paris; presumably because the poisoner had not had access to him there. It was a shame the doctor hadn't diagnosed antifreeze poisoning. And yet, why would he? The symptoms were very similar to those of the flu, which was prevalent at this time of year. Had the doctor suspected, he could have prescribed Antizol, an antidote to ethylene glycol. Rex had prosecuted a murder a few years ago where one teaspoon a day of the poison over a period of ten days had proved lethal. "Do you happen to know what his GP prescribed?" he asked Cheryl.

"No, but there's something else... Lydia describes an incident where they're both watching telly and Tom fell asleep."

"I remember you telling me that. And?"

"Well, I kept my TV guide from Christmas and looked up the programme they'd been watching, and discovered it was about a murderer in the States lacing green jelly with antifreeze."

"Jell-O, as they call it over there."

"That entry is from the third of January. A friend of mine remembered watching that true crime episode while staying over at her sister's."

"And you think someone watching the same show might have derived the idea of antifreeze poisoning?" Rex asked.

"Well, it is a bit of a coincidence, isn't it, that it was aired just before Tom became ill?"

Rex agreed that it was. "Now, going back to

their last night, can you remember anything from your phone conversation with Lydia after the family returned from Chatsworth House that you may have omitted to tell me before?"

"She just said they were all exhausted. Tom was ill and she had driven them home. She joked she was about ready for another drink. That's when she dropped the phone and I heard Tom make a remark. That's the last I ever heard from her," Cheryl said with a sob in her voice.

"You mentioned before about Tom making a joke. Can you remember what he said?"

"It sounded like, 'What's your poison, sweetheart?' There was a piano plinking in the background, I think coming from the TV, so I could have misheard."

Then Tom must have been in the foreground, between the TV and Lydia, Rex surmised. "Do you know what Lydia was drinking?" he asked.

"Probably wine."

"Not Absinthe?" Rex had noticed the almost empty bottle in Tom's study.

"It's possible. She was drinking that at Tom's birthday party. Why?"

"Absinthe is the colour of antifreeze."

"You think someone added antifreeze to the bottle?"

"Or her drink. And to Tom's, perhaps."

"But who?"

"Someone with a strong enough motive," Rex replied, before asking carefully, "And where were you when you made the call to Lydia at around six?"

"In Aston-on-Trent. I go most Sundays to visit my parents for church and Sunday dinner." Cheryl sounded a touch defensive.

Aston-on-Trent was a village about half an hour's drive from Barley Close. It was where he and Helen had attended the macabre wedding.

"You can ask my parents," Cheryl told him. "And I'm sure the detectives checked my mobile phone records and verified the local tower where the signal would have bounced off. I called Lydia just before I set off back to Derby on the off-chance she might want to do something later, but she was too tired, and so I went straight home."

Rex could tell by her huffy tone he had offended her, but it was hard to pursue an investigation without stepping on a few toes. As someone closest to one of the victims, Cheryl could not be ruled out as a suspect. Lydia had dropped her friend and business partner to join the Gladstone furniture company. Cheryl couldn't have been happy about that. Nor did the phone alibi account for the crucial period of time between six and eight, when Natalie had alerted the police upon finding her ex-husband and Lydia dead. "I just had to confirm," he apologized to the young woman. "It would be remiss of me to leave any stone unturned."

"Well, you're barking up the wrong tree," she snapped, retorting with a cliché of her own and cancelling the phone connection.

Rex terminated the call at his end. That had not gone very well, he reflected with discomfort, but it proved the young woman had more spirit than she had hitherto shown.

~EIGHTEEN~

Rex rejoined Helen on the couch and took up the mug of tea she had placed for him on the table. "I wish I could see the blasted diary for myself," he lamented. "Cheryl insists it doesn't contain anything incriminating about anyone. She says Lydia used it more as a factual daily record and that it doesn't delve deeply into matters of the heart. She writes about what she did with Rob, but not, apparently, how she felt about him. Or how she felt about her husband. She refers to his illness and describes everything they saw in Paris, but doesn't give any indication that she's angry with him about his affair with Natalie, whom she doesn't mention by name, or that she wants to leave him, or anything of the sort. Makes me wonder why Lydia would have been so concerned her best friend should have it if something happened to her. And why would a healthy young woman anticipate something happening to her?"

He shook his head. "Anyway, apart from

Uncle Rob, there's nothing much to hide, that I can fathom, without seeing the diary for myself. And I think she may have wanted everyone to know about her affair, to embarrass Tom."

Helen leant back on the sofa with a sigh. "We all knew about Rob and Lydia. If that's all there was to hide, why would Cheryl be reluctant to show it to you?"

Rex shook his head slowly. "All we have to go by are what we've been told by interested parties and what we've read in the papers."

"Well, let's put our heads together. What do we know for certain?" Helen asked.

"That Lydia and Tom Gladstone are dead, whether intentionally or by accident, and that the poisoning in Tom's case had been going on for some time."

"Probably an inside job," Helen said.

"Aye, it had to have been someone close to the family. Let's consider motive and go down the list." He glanced at Helen to make sure she was a willing participant. She nodded in agreement, legs curled up on the sofa, mug of tea in hand. "I'll call out a suspect, and you present a possible motive," he continued. "Tracy."

"Easy," she responded. "Tracy wanted Tom and his money. Perhaps they were in it together. In Tracy, he had a ready-made mother to step into Lydia's shoes. And I rather think Tracy would have liked those designer shoes."

"Ha! But Tom was having an affair with his ex-wife."

"Maybe it was just for old time's sake. Perhaps Natalie wouldn't leave her new husband. Perhaps he was ready to make Tracy wife number three."

Rex made a dissenting sound. "I spent time with Tracy this afternoon. She's pretty and has a good head on her shoulders, but she cannot match Lydia in wit and elegance, from what I've heard. I don't see her retaining Tom's interest for long."

"Maybe he was looking for someone more submissive than Lydia."

"Tracy might have been in love with him, I'm not denying that. I'm just not convinced it was reciprocated."

"If you say so. But Tom could have been going through his mid-life crisis and been looking for a much younger substitute. Men can be very silly."

Rex smiled at her. "Shall we go on?" he asked.

"By all means."

"Daniel Gladstone."

"Sibling rivalry," Helen answered without hesitation. "His brother presumably made more money. Tom had the seemingly perfect family. And you told me Tom had bullied him growing up."

"I'd be more inclined to go with that theory if Daniel had been the one having the affair with

Lydia and she dumped him."

"Perhaps he was named in Tom's will, and the motive was money."

"Possibly, but chances are Tom left everything to his wife and children."

"Well, what about Rob, then?" Helen asked.

"He's a better prospect, I think, for murdering Tom," Rex agreed. "But Lydia?"

"Perhaps he saw her romantic trip to Paris with Tom as a sign it was over between them."

"And perhaps Lydia had more of a stake in the business than he would have liked. The fruit motif furniture was her idea, after all." Rex mulled over the possibility further.

"He was a pretty regular visitor. I often saw his Porsche go by."

"But was he there the evening they died and did he give Lydia a large dose of antifreeze? Tom is more problematic. It seems his poisoning dated back to the beginning of the year with a spell of remittance when they went to Paris and up until his birthday party a week later."

"Rob wouldn't have had a chance to poison him in Paris," Helen noted.

Rex finished his tea. "I wonder what his alibi is. I'd like to meet with him before I go back to Edinburgh. I'm not sure I can give much more time to the case. I have others piling up in my chambers, which I'm paid to take care off."

"It's a bit of a busman's holiday for you, isn't it?" Helen joked.

"Natalie."

"Oh, are we continuing? Envy," she said when he nodded. "She saw Tom's new life with Lydia and got fed up ferrying Devin back and forth."

"She has a new life too," Rex pointed out, setting down his empty mug. "And she was still seeing Tom, if Paula is to be believed. Perhaps it was the perfect arrangement for both of them."

"But not for Dr. Purvis if he'd known. Perhaps he did."

"The deadly dentist." Rex smiled in amusement. "It's just possible his jolliness is a façade. Did you know there's an elevated rate of suicide among dentists?"

"Really? Why is that?"

"Perhaps because they don't get to interact much with their patients. Or else staring into people's mouths all day is depressing."

"It would depress me," Helen agreed. "But from what Jill said, Dr. Purvis has plenty of interaction with his captive audience."

Rex chuckled. "Cheryl?"

Helen stared at him in surprise. "Well, okay. She's not been entirely forthcoming with the diary. What if Lydia knew a secret Cheryl didn't want known, and that's why Cheryl went to retrieve it; before anyone else could? That might explain why her details of its contents are so sketchy. For example, she didn't mention Tom and Lydia's rows, did she? And yet their direct neighbours heard them."

"When?"

"I don't think anyone heard a big blow-up or anything that Sunday night. But you'd think Lydia would have mentioned in her diary if she was having arguments with her husband. I mean, it's not inconsequential. If you ask me, Cheryl's been very selective with what she's told you."

"Arguments between married couples are normal, especially when affairs are involved. If Madame Mathilde is right concerning restless spirits, Lydia and Tom are not having a very good time of it even now."

He saw Helen was tired and decided there had been enough theorizing for one night. He could not, in any case, think of anyone left to round off the list of possible suspects. He felt the parents of the victims could be excluded for now, even if Paula Simmons was a gold-digging piece of work.

They were about to go upstairs to bed when the doorbell rang.

"It's a bit late for someone to be calling round," Helen said, glancing at the carriage clock on the mantelpiece.

"I'll get it." Rex rose from the sofa and went to answer the door. No one was there, but across the street he spied a lanky man in dark leather mount a small motorbike, rev up, and take off with the engine whining. Rex stepped onto the path and could not see anyone else on the dimly lit street. As he turned to go back in the house, he noticed a folded up plastic bag by the door. When he picked it up, he felt something soft inside, itself containing a slim object, harder to the touch. He took the bag inside and closed the front door.

"Who was it?" Helen asked from the hallway.

"I don't know. The only person I saw was a motorcyclist wearing a full-face helmet and those black moon boots. But I found this on the doorstep."

He switched on the lamp on the phone table and looked inside the generic shopping bag. He pulled out a wad of fine snow-white cotton and unfolded it to reveal an amber-coloured tube capped with a rubber top, such as one might use to administer eye drops, and large enough to contain a teaspoon-full of liquid.

"It reminds me of the pipettes we used in school chemistry experiments," Helen said, eying it closely. "But those were clear glass. This looks like acrylic, and it appears to be part of a bottle."

Rex examined the lace-trimmed handkerchief it was wrapped in and caught a whiff of fragrance. "This is embroidered with the letter L," he noted.

"It's very fancy." Helen took a closer look. "I

know that rose-scented perfume. It's *Joie de vivre.* That's what Lydia wore."

"And Cheryl," Rex reminded her.

"Do you think...," Helen trailed off, staring up into Rex's face.

His thumb and forefinger draped in the white material, Rex held up the dropper by its rubber end. "I think we just found the murder weapon," he announced.

~NINETEEN~

Eureka, Rex thought. Something tangible, at last, but why now? After a mere moment's hesitation, he called Cheryl and, after apologizing profusely for the late hour and for upsetting her earlier, he came right out and asked, "Did you drop something off at Helen's just now?"

"Like what?" Cheryl asked, sounding stunned. "What do you mean?"

"Where are you?"

"At my office, making a copy of the diary."

"Why?"

Cheryl paused for a second before speaking. "I've decided to hand it over to the police, like you asked." She told Rex she had fretted all day, but finally decided she could not shoulder the responsibility for what might be a key piece of evidence alone.

"And you're keeping a copy for yourself."

"Yes. I think it's best. What was I supposed to have dropped off?" she repeated.

"Did Lydia have any handkerchiefs embroidered with her first initial?"

"She did. She got them in Paris and gave me three with the letter C on them. Not that I use them, but they're nice to have."

"Listen, Cheryl. If you know who dropped it off at my door, you must tell me."

"Stop accusing me! I didn't, I tell you! Why would I? And I wasn't anywhere near her house the night she was poisoned."

Her outrage sounded genuine, and nor did she betray knowledge of the dispenser found wrapped in the handkerchief. "Well, I'd like to know just who delivered it," he backed down.

"Well, so would I!" Cheryl swore softly on the phone.

"It's just that it has Lydia's perfume on it, the one you wear as well."

"I don't like this. I don't like it one little bit! It's creepy. What's Helen going to do when you go back to Edinburgh? She must be scared stiff. I wouldn't want to be home alone with strangers leaving dead people's stuff at my door. When are you returning to Edinburgh?"

"Tomorrow. Cheryl, just do me a huge favour, please, and make me a copy of the diary as well." He told her it was now all the more imperative that he see the journal. Without it, he was just floundering in the dark and no one could be cleared. And no one was safe.

The next morning, she graciously dropped the copied diary off on her way to work. Rex, unsure up until that moment whether she would deliver the pages, and heartily relieved when she did, assured her he would exercise the utmost discretion. "And you'll give the police the original without delay?" he asked.

"I'm going to say Lydia left it in my car for safe-keeping. I don't want to have to explain I went into their house to retrieve it. Okay, have to run," she exclaimed, turning back down the path.

He leafed through the stapled pages and saw that whole paragraphs had been redacted. "Cheryl, what's this?" he called after her from the front door before she could get in her white Volvo.

"I just edited out the bits about Rob and Lydia's assignations."

"I didn't need a censored edition!" he returned. "At my age, I've seen and heard it all."

Cheryl grinned at him. "Bet you haven't," she said.

"I'm a prosecutor. You don't think I'm familiar with all manner of perversions?"

The young woman appeared to make an effort not to laugh. "I suppose. But you seem so…"

"Staid?" he demanded.

"Buttoned-up?" Cheryl bit her lip as if reluctant to offend him. "But I swear there's nothing important left out."

Rex expelled a deep breath. "Well, thanks anyway," he said, brandishing the sheaf of pages in the air.

"Is that the copy of the diary?" Helen asked, coming out of the kitchen as he was closing the front door.

"The PG version. Cheryl saw fit to protect my sensibilities by blacking out the naughty parts about Lydia and Rob. He's older than I am. If he can do it, surely I can read about it!"

Helen let out a peal of laughter. "She must think you're an old fuddy-duddy. It's really quite sweet!"

"And completely misguided," he reminded his fiancée.

While she finished getting ready for work upstairs, he drank another cup of tea at the kitchen table. A disjointed picture was beginning to form in his mind, and one thing was apparent: The deaths had been no accident. Tom had been the victim of chronic poisoning, quite possibly aided by a dropper. And the person who had delivered it knew something.

Suicide was even less likely. From what he had learnt, neither Tom nor Lydia had been the type. Presumably, the police had reached the same conclusions, which was why the case was still open; and might remain so without the diary—and the dropper. He would need to hand it over. Their forensics lab could test for traces of ethylene glycol.

He planned to meet with Rob Gladstone before catching the train back to Edinburgh. The uncle was the last link in the chain with Tom's parents away in Berkshire. Rex had spoken with everyone else closest to the victims.

Helen didn't have to be at the school until later in the morning and said she would run a few errands while he was at Fruité Furniture, and then take him to the station.

The premises were around the corner from where he had met Daniel for coffee the previous week. The street's white stripes, designating its use for pedestrian traffic, swept in a long curve flanked by tall buildings, one side more modern than the other, and each containing shops or offices at ground level. People hurried to get to their places of work by nine. Rex located the Fruité Furniture headquarters in one of the older buildings embellished with arched windows and ornate, ruddy-hued brickwork on the upper storey façades.

He crossed a lobby promoting the trademark armchairs, and approached the front desk, where a sallow young man prematurely balding on top lifted his head to greet him.

"I was hoping to have a brief word with Mr. Robert Gladstone."

"He's at the factory and then he'll be conducting interviews all day," the man in shirt and tie explained in a regretful tone.

Rex had done his research and knew the factory that produced the furniture was a converted mill on the outskirts of Derby. "Interviewing for which position?" he asked with casual interest.

"Sales Director and Marketing Director."

"Key personnel. Replacements for Tom and Lydia Gladstone?"

"Right." The young man cut him a sharp look. His gaze fell to Rex's business attire visible beneath the dark brown overcoat, as though to determine whether the visitor was from the Inland Revenue or else some other red-tape institution, and how best to fob him off in light of his employer's busy schedule. "Can I make an appointment for you next week?"

"I'm heading back to Edinburgh this morning."

"I'm afraid Mr. Gladstone's been rushed off his feet since he got back from the furniture fair in Munich. A ton of orders to fill. And, of course, the two positions," the receptionist trailed off in apology.

Rex was at least able to elicit the dates of the trip. The five days in Germany spanned the weekend the Gladstone couple had been poisoned, and Rob, it seemed, had had a full schedule that entire week, no doubt verified by the police. Rex was about to leave when he had a further thought. "I suppose—"

The phone at reception rang, interrupting him, and the young man lifted a finger, motioning for him to wait briefly while he answered the call. He expressed a formal and friendly greeting and, with a "Just one second, I'll put you through," transferred the caller. He looked back up at Rex with an attentive expression.

"I suppose the police searched Tom and Lydia Gladstones' offices?" Rex finished what he had been about to say.

"They did."

"Removed laptops and personal items?" Rex queried the male receptionist.

"You're late!" he admonished a young woman hastening towards them from the main entrance, where other people were still arriving singly and in pairs.

"My bus was," she responded, short of breath, her bosom jiggling as she removed her coat on her way across the lobby.

With a stern look, the man relinquished his swivel chair to her and walked around the side of the desk to join Rex. He stood half a foot shorter than the Scotsman who also eclipsed him in bulk. "Sorry. As you were saying…"

"The police," Rex said in a low voice, so the female receptionist would not hear.

"Right. I led them to the offices in question. I'm the building manager," he explained. "Lydia Gladstone always locked her door, so I had to open it with a duplicate key."

"Why did she lock her office?" Rex asked. "Is that unusual here?" It wasn't a high-tech company, after all, or one that housed sensitive records.

"I expect it was because she kept some of her jewellery in there. I saw it being removed, and it looked like she had some expensive shelf ornaments as well. Or, more like dressing table ornaments. I suppose she must have changed at the office sometimes. She had asked me to install a full-length mirror at the back of the door. She was a bit of a clothes-horse. Very nicely dressed," the building manager added quickly to soften the note of criticism. "Why do you ask?" he enquired with a politely puzzled expression.

"Some valuables allegedly went missing from her house," Rex told him.

"Ah." The building manager smiled and nodded. "You're an insurance investigator. I thought you might be something like that. Best bet would be to check with the police."

"Aye, it might," Rex agreed evasively. He thanked the young man and bid him good day. A fruitful visit to Fruité Furniture, he congratulated himself.

After he left the building, he searched on his phone for photos of the fair in Munich, and found one with none other than Rob Gladstone standing in front of his booth, proudly holding up a framed award. Eliminate Uncle Rob, he concluded, not wholly undeterred. His alibi only served to substantiate his predominant theory.

Helen reached her car in the parking lot minutes after he did. "How did it go?" she asked.

"I couldn't get in to see Gladstone, but it's of no consequence, since he was on business in Germany when Tom and Lydia were poisoned." Rex opened the driver's-side door for her. "Did you get everything done?"

"I went to the bank and dropped off the dry cleaning. I can do the rest later. Let's get you to the station. There's a lot of traffic and you don't want to miss your train."

On the way, Rex received a call from the legal colleague he had asked to look into Larry Leath's background. Nothing much to report on the vacuum cleaner salesman, he was told: One arrest as a student at a protest rally in Edinburgh opposing spy satellites in space; now lived in a flat over his appliance repair shop in Derby with his wife of thirty years.

"You remember Jill's Hoover salesman?" he said to Helen as he slipped his phone back in his pocket. "He might be a bit of a crackpot, but he's apparently harmless. However, the curious thing is he told me Tracy was wearing sapphire earrings and a diamond on her ring finger when he visited the Gladstone house. And some of Lydia's jewellery and other valuables turned up in Lydia's office. What do you make of that?"

"I think quite a bit could be made of that," Helen replied.

~TWENTY~

Rex said his farewells to Helen outside the terminal and promised to call that same evening. The high-speed train bound for Waverley Station was waiting on the tracks, but he had almost fifteen minutes to spare, enough time to call Tracy.

She didn't answer. He left an urgent message on her voicemail and paced the platform with his briefcase and bag, impatient for her call. Five more minutes passed. The last passengers were boarding. His phone rang.

"Tracy, I know it was you," he said without preamble. "You would possibly know where Helen lives and you had access to Lydia's personal items."

"I'm not the only one. Try Goldilocks."

"Goldilocks? You mean Cheryl?"

"She was always at the house."

"I spoke to Cheryl. It wasn't her. Why did you have someone leave that bag at Helen's door?"

He heard a sigh of resignation. "I found the dropper in Lydia's medicine cabinet hidden behind a roll of makeup removal pads."

"What were you doing looking in her medicine cabinet?" he asked.

"I wasn't snooping, if that's what you're thinking. Hannah had an ear infection. I was looking for the homeopathic treatment we used. She was very prone to them last year, but hadn't had an infection in a while."

"The dropper was from that bottle?"

"I think so, but I couldn't find the bottle anywhere." Tracy paused before adding, "I told Tom about it. I went to see him at his office after Lydia got home that last Friday."

"Why?"

"I had my suspicions. I saw her tampering with his medicine once. I'm not sure what she was doing exactly because I only saw the hand that was holding the bottle. The other was hidden by the cabinet door. Then, when I found the dropper, but the ear ointment missing, well, I just thought I should warn him. I didn't know about the antifreeze then. I'd just never known him to be ill before January, and I'd been working for them a whole year by then."

A whistle blew urgently.

"What did Tom say?" Rex yelled above the sudden whoosh and rumble of the train preparing to depart.

"He laughed. Then he looked thoughtful, then

he went pale. I wrapped the dropper in one of her hankies and hid it in my bag to use as evidence if necessary. I was convinced she was up to something. I was trying to protect Tom."

Rex deposited his bag and briefcase on the concrete platform and opened the door to the carriage. He pushed his baggage inside and followed. "Why didn't you tell me about this yesterday?" he asked standing by the open door.

A guard slammed it shut.

"My mom said not to get involved, but she did it. I know she did. Lydia, I mean. I want justice for Tom, and I don't think Hannah or anyone else should take the blame, even if Lydia killed herself too."

It was getting harder to hear Tracy over the drone of the train, which suddenly lurched forward and then juddered to a stop just as abruptly, catching him off balance. He braced himself against the door with his free arm, wondering about the delay.

"I asked my friend Pete to drop the bag off at your fiancée's house anonymously...," Tracy's voice dwindled in his ear.

After a semi-inaudible exchange of goodbyes, Rex cut the phone connection. He found the compartment half empty and relatively quiet. Few tourists travelled to Edinburgh at this time of year, and this morning he spotted mostly single passengers on business or those visiting family, most of them plugged into laptops and smartphones.

He placed his weekend bag in the overhead rack and settled into his seat with his briefcase beside him. As he glanced out the grimy window he saw a familiar figure hurry past on the platform in the company of an overweight woman, both of them towing small suitcases on wheels and franticly gesticulating at the train. Rex pressed himself back against the seat in a desperate attempt to avoid detection. When the pair disappeared from sight and, minutes later, had not appeared in his carriage, he began to relax.

The coincidence of running into Leath the first time had been fortuitous, but twice was too much of a good thing. Rex had no doubt the salesman would have hailed his fellow countryman and plonked himself down with his wife within speaking distance. His sort never allowed silence to interrupt their words, and Rex had plenty enough to occupy his time for the next four hours, not least Lydia's diary, which he held in his hands.

The train pulled out of the station, gathering speed. He had made this trip so many times that the industrial suburbs and low, undulating hills of the Derbyshire countryside beyond the window were a familiar sight. He watched in a state of apprehensive anticipation, wondering whether the pages would contain further revelations or else jumble and contradict the pieces of the puzzle he had painstakingly assembled in his head.

Without further prevarication, he opened the diary and began reading Lydia's entries from the first of the year, and did not stop until he reached the final one written the day before she died. Cheryl had not exaggerated the overall detached nature of the journal. Had he not been looking for hidden clues, he would have found the non-edited passages less than enthralling.

He remembered the wrapped sandwiches and thermos of coffee Helen had packed in his bag and stood to get them. The fleeting view of fields and pastures from the windows was now obscured by a persistent grey drizzle. Some of the passengers slept, lulled by the thrum of the train. He sat back down and ate his lunch while ruminating whether Lydia had kept journals before she started this one. He decided it was unlikely. The purpose of the diary, he now saw, was to lay the groundwork for her cold-blooded crime.

She had fictionalized her life with Tom, not disclosing the arguments between them for the simple reason that marital discord would show motive. Nor did she harp on about his affair or name the other woman, for the same reason.

She chronicled Tom's "flu" to account for his symptoms of poisoning. To anyone who later questioned those symptoms, she would have insisted the doctor had said he had influenza. Rex further surmised it would have been suspicious for him to die alone with his wife at a Paris hotel and inconvenient having to deal with a death in a foreign country. Consequently, Lydia had held off on his regimen of antifreeze for the duration and waited to resume until after his birthday party, where everyone would see them as a happily married couple recently returned from their second honeymoon.

Thereafter, Tom had succumbed once more to his symptoms and was no doubt back on his tainted medicine, with the fatal dose of antifreeze possibly slipped into the ice cream the family ate upon returning from their outing to Chatsworth. Lydia, in her mind, was giving him his just desserts for getting back to his first wife. Not satisfied with cheating on him with his uncle, she had wanted him dead as well. The keying of the intern's car had shown what a vindictive vixen she was.

Rex closed the diary. There remained one piece of the puzzle to slot into place.

~TWENTY-ONE~

At his chambers in Edinburgh, Rex made a call to a barrister friend in Derby, who in turn contacted the Gladstone family solicitor. It transpired that Tom had changed his will two days before his death and left half of everything to his first wife and mother of his son, and the other half in trust to Hannah for when she came of age, thereby disinheriting Lydia.

"Must have been a reason for that," the friend remarked after reporting the terms of the will.

"She was trying to kill him," Rex said. "What better reason?"

Lydia might have ended up poisoning Rob Gladstone as well. Why not, if she had managed to get away with the murder of her first spouse?

"Perhaps the couple should have tried marriage counselling?" his acquaintance said facetiously before ringing off at his end.

The news of the will only confirmed to Rex that Tom had finally discovered what his wife was planning. Subsequently, he had taken precautions to safeguard his personal assets, if not his life. He might have started criminal and divorce proceedings once he had proof of her treachery, but he never got the chance.

Rex phoned Cheryl and commended her for her accurate account of the diary's contents. He felt Lydia had underestimated her friend's loyalty and had expected her to report the diary to the police sooner in the event of Tom's death. Of course, Lydia had not anticipated her own demise. Had Cheryl kept quiet about the journal, Rex had no doubt Lydia would have left it in a place where it would be found, without being too obvious about it.

He told Cheryl the diary served to prove she had no motive to kill Tom and to cast suspicion on Tracy, who had a fondness for Lydia's possessions. The valuables found in Lydia's office were presumably the items missing from the house and reported stolen to the police. Lydia had been framing the nanny for Tom's death, hinting at unrequited love as a motive. "That," he explained to Cheryl, "was how she had hoped to get away with murder."

Cheryl sounded devastated by the notion her friend could have manipulated her and murdered her husband. Never in a million years would she have guessed the truth, she said when she had heard the story, and which Rex asked her to keep under wraps for now. He would tell her the rest later.

He called his fiancée and asked if it would be convenient if he headed down to Derby on Thursday, providing he had cleared his desk by then. "We could make a long weekend of it," he added.

"Of course!" she said. "What brought this on? No, don't tell me! Something came up in the diary…"

"The Paris trip was a smokescreen, as was Tom's flu," he briefly explained. "Ever since the company Christmas party, when Lydia's affair with her wealthy boss began, she planned on getting rid of her husband. In the end, her web of deceit cost her her own life."

"But I still don't see…," Helen began.

"There are still a few loose ends to tie up. I want to see Paula Simmons and Daniel in person, out of courtesy."

The public scandal of mutual murder and adulterous motives would be hard to bear and also bad for the family business, but Rex was convinced it was better for the victims' nearest and dearest to know the truth than to live with doubt and suspicion, even if the truth was as unpalatable as poison.

Rex regretted in his last private case writing to

the police about his findings instead of confronting the killer and trying to extract a confession, especially since he had known the person in question. However, in this instance, there was no danger to weigh against a sense of obligation, or so he perceived at the time.

~TWENTY-TWO~

When Rex arrived back in Derby later that week, he took a taxi straight from the station to the Fruité Furniture offices. It was not yet noon, and Helen was working.

The bosomy receptionist greeted him with a nod of recognition and a pert smile. "I remember you!"

"I've come to see Daniel Gladstone. Is he free?"

"I'll find out." She fluttered her false eyelashes at him. "Who shall I say?"

"Rex Graves, QC."

She then manipulated the switchboard. "Danny? A Rex Graves to see you. He'll be right down," she told Rex. "So you're a Queen's Counsel! I saw 'Silk' and thought it was fabulous," she said of the TV drama. "Do you wear a wig and gown in court?"

"I do."

The switchboard grew busy of a sudden and

she had to turn her attention back to the phones. Daniel appeared in a casual suit, and she winked at him as she redirected a call. He glanced away, smiling shyly and running a hand through his light brown hair.

"Nice your callers are not given the recorded run-around," Rex said to him.

"Mr. Gladstone wouldn't hear of it. He's very old school."

"A man after my own heart. Can I take you to lunch?"

Daniel glanced at his watch and drew in his breath. "I'd like that, but I can only spare you a quarter of an hour. I have a looming deadline. Do you have new information?"

"Aye, and it's private."

"My cubicle is cluttered with all sorts of tech gear, and there's only the one chair. I'd take you to the conference room, but I'm not an executive here. The break room should be empty for the next thirty minutes." Daniel led him behind the reception area and summoned a lift. Inside, he pressed a button to the third floor, and they rose the short distance in silence. The car pinged to a stop.

"The police have granted the family access to my brother's house," he told Rex as they made their way along a corridor with offices leading off on one side. "I need to get there before that vulture cleans it out."

"I take it you're referring to Paula Simmons."

"Right. She had better not touch Tom's stuff. Here we are," Daniel said, leading him into a small common room equipped with a basic kitchen. He helped himself to coffee from the machine on the table and offered Rex a cup.

When they were seated at the Formica table, Rex explained what he had discovered about Lydia's involvement in Tom's death, including the dropper Tracy had found and his affair with his ex-wife.

"So, not an accident?" Daniel asked in dismay.

Rex shook his head. "Means, motive, and opportunity. There was one person who had ready access to Tom's medicine and food, and that was his spouse. And let's not forget the life insurance incentive. Lydia may have hoped to cash in on a considerable amount. Any idea how much?"

"No idea."

"Hundreds of thousands of pounds, I imagine. Enough, no doubt, to at least pay off the mortgage on their house, which is a concern for most people if a working spouse dies."

"So her motive was money?" Daniel asked.

"Money, greed, revenge... The usual."

"Well, not saying that Tom deserved to die, not saying that at all; just that he should have been more careful of people's feelings. Bad karma.

Know what I mean?"

Rex nodded slowly. "He must have hurt Lydia very badly."

"But none of this explains how she died. Was that an accident?"

Rex had been preparing for this moment. He took a deep breath. "Daniel, I regret to tell you your brother is not blameless in the crime either. Unless Lydia suffered belated qualms of conscience about murdering him and poisoned herself in an act of contrition, it appears he poisoned her."

"Are you sure?" Daniel stared at Rex, his mouth ajar.

"He changed his will. And Cheryl recalls overhearing him on the phone saying, 'What's your poison, sweetheart?' shortly before they both died." Tom must have been standing close, perhaps close enough to force the Absinthe down his wife's throat... "They watched a true crime programme in January about antifreeze poisoning," Rex continued. "Presumably your brother had been paying more attention than Lydia supposed. He finally realized what she was up to and gave her a hefty dose of her own medicine—before it was too late."

"Dear God," Daniel murmured, his face as white as the walls surrounding them. "But he acted in self-defence, right?" His gaze fell to his mug of coffee, which he pushed aside. "Poor Hannah. And Devin. What now?"

"The case is circumstantial and might not even hold up in court if either party were still alive. Yet, as far as I'm concerned, it's the only logical conclusion to be drawn. The police may come up with something different, but I'll be taking the dropper to the station later today." Rex had just finished speaking when he received a call from Jill on his phone.

"Just thought you'd like to know Paula Simmons is back at the Gladstone house," Helen's friend and neighbour informed him.

"Thanks, I'll be right over. I wanted to talk to her." He looked across the table at Daniel, who held his head in his hands. "The vulture has landed," he said, preparing once more to be the bearer of bad news.

~TWENTY-THREE~

Rex took a taxi to Helen's house, where he dropped off his briefcase and bag inside the door, before hurrying on to the Gladstone residence.

The Mercedes Benz was parked outside, the police tape had been removed. After ringing the front door bell to no avail, he walked into the spacious hallway and called out "Hello?" across the marble floors. "Paula?"

He had not seen the house in daylight and noticed for the first time the plush cherry sofa in the curve of the staircase and a large rubber plant in a brass urn. It felt as chilly indoors as outside.

"Up here," Paula's voice travelled down to him.

He mounted the stairs and halted outside a door, where an assortment of small furniture had been assembled: tripod tables, wrought-iron lampstands, Italian statuettes in stone, and other transportable items. He poked his head around the door and found Paula folding items of clothing in a gaping suitcase on the king-size canopy bed.

"I'm glad I caught you," he said. "I wanted to talk to you about what I found out in the course of my investigation. I'm afraid it may not be what you want to hear."

"Well, nothing's going to bring her back, is it?" Paula fetched a fur-lined coat from a large wardrobe and came out of the bedroom and placed it over the banister. She was on her way back to the bedroom when Rex addressed her again, more sternly this time.

"Mrs. Simmons, I have reason to believe your daughter was responsible for Tom's death, and he hers." He explained about the dropper and medicine and the elaborate lengths Lydia had gone to in her diary to absolve herself of any wrongdoing. "And she set her nanny up for his murder by, among other things, claiming valuables had disappeared from this house."

"What valuables?" Paula demanded, facing him on the landing. "Not her sapphires and pearls, or gold necklace and bracelet. I have all that."

"Items she took to her office, and which are now in police custody."

"Will I get them back?"

Rex made an effort to curb his exasperation. He had just accused her daughter of murder, and all she appeared concerned about was Lydia's jewellery. "At some point," he said. "But as far as the life insurance, I think it could become extremely litigious."

"Litigious?"

"A drawn-out legal dispute."

"Drawn-out?" Paula repeated, pouncing on the word.

"The insurance policy on Tom might be voided altogether. Murderers are precluded from benefitting monetarily from their crimes, and this might apply to their estate, in Lydia's case, you, if the insurer found out what really happened."

Paula had grown pale. "I won't get a penny?"

"It could further be argued she was instrumental in her own death," he added. "In which case, Hannah might get nothing from Tom's side. It could get complicated. You might want to consult with an insurance lawyer."

"And how much will *that* cost me?" Paula riled. "It would be money down the drain if I don't win." She glared at him as if he were the enemy. "And the insurance company will have a better lawyer than I could ever afford."

"Insurance companies will try to hold on to their funds at all costs," Rex agreed.

"Then I'm sunk!" Paula cried, her face crumpling and turning a mottled red beneath her pale makeup. "Why didn't the selfish little cow just divorce him? Now I'm raising my granddaughter on my own, and I scarcely make enough from the salon to scrape by."

While Rex listened in stupefaction to her tirade, he became aware of someone outside the front door turning the brass knob.

"Have you spoken to the police?" Paula demanded.

"Not yet."

"The tabloids and talk shows will have a field day!" she cried in alarm, unaware of what was happening downstairs, with Rex's bulk blocking her view of the front door.

Beneath her heated words he heard the door ease open and turned his head to see who it was. In that instant, Daniel burst through, shouting, "Look out!"

Rex, glancing back, ducked in time to avoid a wrought-iron lampstand striking his neck, but he lost his balance and crashed into the twisted wood banister, which gave way under his weight. His feet left the landing as he slipped through the broken railings. He grabbed on to an intact pole at the last moment and, swinging in the air fourteen feet above the marble floor of the hallway, doubted it would hold. Paula lifted the upside-down lampstand above her head in both hands and bore down hard on him.

"Jump!" Daniel yelled over the scrape of furniture below. Peeking down, Rex released his grasp just as the iron base connected with the remaining section of balcony and cleaved the railing in two. Rex landed on the spongy sofa, his knees buckling.

He reached down and steadied himself. Daniel helped him to the floor. "One of yours?" Rex asked.

Daniel nodded. "Sturdy product, yeah? Saved you from breaking some bones."

"Could have been my neck," Rex said, examining the red imprints of twisted pole on his sweaty palms. "Thank you." He pulled the young man towards the front door, in case the madwoman on the landing decided to aim something at them, but when he looked up she had disappeared. Daniel must have scared her off.

"She tried to kill you," the young man said. "Why?"

"She thought if the police found out what I've ascertained about Lydia and Tom's deaths, the life insurance carrier won't pay out. Not to mention the salacious scandal that would erupt."

"Well, I'm calling the police now." Daniel did so, supplying the necessary details and urging them to hurry since he had no idea what the assailant might do next.

"Should we wait until they arrive or go up and apprehend her?" Rex asked Daniel. He could hear Paula sobbing hysterically upstairs.

"The police said not to attempt to approach

her. And I don't think she'd get far if she tried to escape. Especially with a flat tyre." Daniel drew a large building nail from his suit pocket. "I knew the blood-sucking parasite would try to make off with everything she could get her hands on, so I came prepared."

"She's made a good start judging by the pile upstairs."

"Are you sure she didn't murder Tom and Lydia herself?" Daniel asked.

Rex shook his head. "I'm sure. For one thing, I don't think she planned to bring Hannah up on her own."

"She's not fit to! Natalie can take Hannah, and she can grow up with her half-brother. That's a far better arrangement. I mean, look how Lydia turned out!"

Happy families, Rex thought cynically, looking about the elegant entrance hall as the wail of a police siren grew progressively louder. The Gladstone case had been a complex one. The victim had turned murderer and the murderer had ultimately become a victim. In the end, both husband and wife had complied with their wedding vows, being parted only by death. But perhaps death had not parted them yet, and their spirits were still at war in the house on Barley Close.

A Rex Graves Mini-Mystery

SAY MURDER
~ WITH ~
FLOWERS

C. S. CHALLINOR

*

Rex Graves stood by in a dark grey suit, watching the proceedings. The mourners would in all likelihood take the bulky, bearded redhead to be an usher or an assistant to the funeral home's director, which suited his purpose for now.

First in line went the parents, shrunk in grief, Sir William Howes extending a comforting arm around his wife's fragile shoulders. The viewing casket, nestled among the floral arrangements and formal wreaths, enveloped the body of Elise Howes, struck down in the bloom of youth as she carried home a bunch of yellow chrysanthemums, subsequently found strewn across New Bond Street. Muted sobs punctuated the chilled silence as the small gathering passed in single file before the coffin lined with cream satin. The women in black veils, the men sombrely attired, contrasted with the white lilies, gerberas and roses.

The deceased's father, adamant Elise's death had been no accident and entertaining a suspicion of murder, had given his solicitor *carte blanche* to retain the services of a private investigator. In view of Rex's success in solving murder mysteries, Mr. Whitmore had prevailed upon the Scottish barrister to solve this most distressing of cases. The hit-and-run driver had not been found. CCTV cameras had failed to record the incident, and no eye witnesses had come

166

forward, except for a man exiting a nightclub in a neighbouring street. He had heard a car rev up—a sports car, judging by the throaty pitch of the engine—followed by a thud, a whining protest of acceleration and, finally, a squeal of tires as the vehicle careened around the corner, with only the taillights visible as the reveller reached the scene. The young woman had been dragged a few feet beneath the vehicle and abandoned on the road.

According to the eye witness, the victim's last gasping words before losing consciousness had been "Chris" and "Jean," or maybe "Jen." She had died in the ambulance. A passer-by had noticed a grey van among the cars parked on the street where the accident occurred. And now Sir William Howes, a cabinet minister described in political circles as ruthless and intractable, was most anxious to bring the culprit to justice, whomever it was.

Rex had agreed to adjust his schedule in Edinburgh and taken the train from Waverley Station to London. He had met briefly with Sir Howes at his Belgravia home before reaching the funeral parlour in time to take his first glimpse of the deceased's nearest and dearest, previously described to him in detail by the meticulous Mr. Whitmore.

*

Passing presently under Rex's review as she paid her respects was Elise's business partner, a luscious brunette, most becoming in her mourning suit. Eyes obscured by a gauzy veil covering half her face, full lips trembling with emotion, she placed a rosebud in the casket. Shannon Smythe was not quite the femme fatale Whitmore had suggested, perhaps. Still, who could resist such a woman? An old fogey like himself, for starters, Rex reasoned. But where there was a beautiful woman there was usually drama.

And drama in its ultimate manifestation—murder—was his hobby, as well as forming a large part of his prosecutorial work at the High Court of Justiciary in Scotland's capital.

Upon first hearing the shortlist of suspects, he thought the cabinet minister might be jumping to conclusions, his mind unhinged by sorrow at the untimely death of his daughter. The family solicitor had gone on to explain that the Howes girl was wealthy in her own right. Her business venture, *Head Start!,* had taken off since Will and Kate's Royal Wedding, when the creative array of hats and "fascinators," such as those worn by the daughters of the Duchess of York, had caught the public's attention. The Queen's Diamond Jubilee had only served to reinforce the craze, as would, no doubt, the christening of the new prince.

Elise and her founding partner, Shannon

Smythe, a friend from the London School of Design, had capitalized on the national historic events and signed lucrative deals with higher-end department stores to supply head gear riffed off top designers. Not a coincidence, Rex's legal colleague had emphasized, that Elise should be "got rid of" to benefit Shannon, especially since the partner's alibi had proved to be pure fiction. The girl might well have something to hide, said Mr. Whitmore, speaking on behalf of Sir Howes.

Sir Howes' reasons for suspecting Ms. Smythe stemmed from her flimsy alibi for Friday night, subsequently disproved by the police; and the fact she drove a silver Fiat 500. The gold-plated buckle on Elise's shoulder bag, recovered intact at the scene, had been scraped and flecked with silver paint. Yet only a few minor dents and scratches had been found on Ms. Smythe's front bumper, and there was no evidence of a touch-up. That she had lied to police about the film she'd seen at the West End cinema was more revealing. She had given a synopsis of the plot, only to be informed that the movie was not yet showing in the UK, and she must have based her recollections on the preview. She had responded, with a shrug, that she'd stayed home painting her toe nails, listening to Adele on her iPod, and had from then on refused to budge from her story.

Rex was intrigued by her reaction to being

outed, as relayed by the solicitor. After all, a shrug denoted something less urgent to hide than a hit-and-run. He was determined to find out more than the police had unearthed. His sympathetic approach and Lowland Scots burr invariably produced a tongue-loosening effect on people, particularly women, and in his usual garb of tweed jacket and corduroys, he cut a far less imposing figure than in the black gown and stiff wig he wore for court.

Regarding who had given Elise Howes the chrysanthemums, the solicitor was uncertain. Elise, working late at her office that Friday night, was presumed to be meeting her fiancé at *Presto's* on Market Street, but had, apparently, been stood up. This accounted for her walking home alone late at night. The fiancé, Gino Giannelli, had denied they'd had a date, even though they frequently met at the bistro for dinner and she often stayed at his flat on weekends. The Italian was Suspect Number Two on Sir Howes' list. He might have been Number One had his daughter already been married to him, citing Elise's family fortune as motive.

The Howes' eldest daughter stood next to her parents receiving the guests. Mr. Whitmore had confided that Jennifer's life goal while awaiting her great aunts' demise—presumably the two desiccated old ladies sitting nearby dressed head to toe in black brocade—was to snag a rich husband and, to this end, she frequented high society sporting events, including Ascot, Wimbledon, and Polo in the Park. A horsey girl, her scarlet mouth showed pinched and stark in a face almost as ghostly pale as her dead sister's. The Howes gene pool had conspired to bestow the worst features of each parent on her person. Unlike her ethereally pretty sibling, Jennifer had inherited her father's prominent nose and long chin, and her mother's toneless blond hair, weighed down in both cases by black cloche hats in crushed velvet.

Rex did not fail to notice that in unguarded moments she eyed, with primal hunger, a designer-stubbled man with mussed up black hair held in place with slick gel, who could be none other than Elise's grieving lover. And Sir Howes' second prime suspect.

"Look into him as well as the girl," the minister had instructed Rex in his gleaming wood library that day.

The machismo Gino Giannelli hung back in a palm-potted corner of the funeral parlour, in conversation with one of Sir Howes' aged aunts, his dark eyes bright with tears as he performed operatic gestures of despair. During his brief visit to Sir Howes' home, Rex had gathered that the Minister of Transport did not altogether approve of the "Italian stud" to begin with, although, given his daughter's track record of broken engagements, he had not been unduly concerned about a finish line at the altar.

Giannelli's work involved the import of luxury Italian cars. "I introduced him to some rich and influential acquaintance who might be in the market for an overpriced pile of foreign metal," Sir William Howes had told Rex, handing him a snifter of brandy from a cut-glass decanter. "He even tried to sell *me* one of his fancy cars. Fat chance. I don't drive these days—I like my drink too much. Darling Elise was no good at controlling her alcohol intake either, or her reaction to it."

Indeed, Rex had learnt from his reliable source, Mr. Whitmore, that the coroner had found her alcohol consumption to be considerably elevated.

"So much safer to use a car service, I thought. Just goes to show," Sir Howes had maundered. "You try to pre-empt disaster, and it happens anyway."

The irony of the Minister of Transport using a private car service had not been lost on Rex, especially since there was no shortage of tube stations in Central London. But Sir Howes was careful enough about his image not to have a personal full-time chauffeur.

His driver of preference from Sloane Car Service was one Erik Christiansen, who now passed impassively by the coffin, black cap in his hands. Tall, with ice- blue eyes, white-blond hair and chiselled features, he was a foil to the muscular Gino Giannelli. He had been in a limo the night in question, waiting to pick up Sir Howes and his wife from a dinner party held in honour of the Italian Ambassador, bachelor-about-town Vittorio Scalfaro, an event that took place at a private club in the vicinity of the accident.

The silver stretch limo in service that night had been found to be in immaculate condition, per the police report provided by Mr. Whitmore. In any case, Sir Howes had come to trust the Danish driver implicitly, and sometimes utilized his services for delivery of time-sensitive documents and other important business.

Gino Giannelli drove a black Lancia, Whitmore had divulged. And the victim's sister, who apparently felt most comfortable on a horse, availed herself of the car service. It seemed both Howes girls eschewed public transport entirely. Rex tried not to hold their snobbishness against them. Elise was dead, and he'd accepted the task of bringing the responsible party, whether a reckless driver or a callous murderer, to justice.

*

With the sum of these facts and the faces fresh in

his mind, Rex took a cab that afternoon to the bistro where Elise Howes was last seen alive. According to staff at Presto's, she had sat alone at the bar sipping chilled limoncellos, alternately checking her phone and anxiously looking around the restaurant. Finally, at around eleven o' clock, she rose from her stool after petulantly paying her tab. Tripping in her high heels on her way out, she grabbed onto a tapestry wall hanging and brought it down on herself, as witnessed by the bartender and a waiter, who rushed to her assistance. They had not thought to send her home in a taxi. A regular, she was generally in the company of Signor Giannelli. No one had thought to call him either. She had simply left, unsteady on her feet, after insisting she'd be fine and pressing another large tip in the hand of the bartender for any damage to the wall and decorative hanging.

When questioned further, no one at Presto's had seen her with the yellow flowers found at the accident, which suggested she had acquired them between leaving the bistro and getting hit by the car, an hour-long interval no one could account for.

Chrysanthemums were an odd choice of flower for a courting man, Rex reflected as he waited under the awning for a lull in the rain; especially for a man like Gino. Rex idly watched the waves of multicolour umbrellas on either side of the street, remembering when he had given an ex-girlfriend a bunch of mums in hospital. She had clearly been disappointed, informing him later, when sufficiently healed emotionally from her suicide attempt, that chrysanthemums symbolized death in certain countries in Europe.

No good deed ever went unpunished, he ruminated. Especially with women. They never told you what they really wanted, and then acted as though you should have been able to read their minds. How was he supposed to understand every nuance and significance behind flowers, whose primary purpose, he'd always thought, were to look nice, smell sweet, and cheer people up?

Had Elise Howes displayed a similar reaction to the flowers? Whom she had met or visited after she left Presto's, if not Gino, remained a mystery following Rex's informal interviews with the staff. Could a woman have given her the chrysanthemums? It wasn't her birthday, he knew from her date of birth listed in his file. Dick Whitmore, who had been in touch with the detectives on the case, had reported a two-minute call on her retrieved mobile phone from her sister Jennifer earlier that fateful evening, and a text message from Shannon Smythe entreating her partner to check out a line of hats featured in the latest edition of *Vogue*. Rex would have liked to talk to the mother, but Lady Howes had taken to her bed after the vigil and was not receiving company. Diana Howes was, as Whitmore described her, "a woman of extremely delicate nerves."

Hailing a cab on the street, Rex gave the driver the address of Elise's flat in Mayfair Mews, and asked if he knew of any flower shops in the area.

"Up 'ere," the cabbie informed him, pointing to a narrow turning as they took off over the wet cobblestones. "Say It with Flowers is the name of it. But it's a one-way street and it'll take us out of our way."

Say It With Flowers, Rex knew from his mother's television viewing, was a nineteen thirties musical about an ailing London flower seller whose fellow stall owners organize a benefit at a local pub to fund her trip to the seaside.

"Is it the only florist near here?" he asked the driver.

"Only one I know of."

"Can you not find a parking space?"

"Chance'd be a fine thing."

Rex asked the cabbie to double back and take him to the shop, regardless. This proved no easy feat in the maze of streets, but finally the manoeuvre was accomplished, and Rex asked him to wait outside while he made enquiries as to who might have purchased yellow chrysanthemums on Friday night. The sales clerk, dressed in a dark green canvas apron, remembered a "dishy foreign bloke what paid cash."

"Stocky build? Dark hair?"

"And with dreamy dark eyes. Drop-dead gorgeous, he was."

Had Elise dropped dead at this charmer's hands? Rex wondered. "What time was this?" he asked.

"We was just closing. Must've been almost midnight. We stay open late Fridays and Saturdays for the theatre crowd."

Rex thanked the young woman and left the shop. Had she gone to Gino's flat to confront him about his standing her up, if such was the case? Had he tried to mollify her with flowers as he walked her back home?

"Wot, no flowers?" The cabbie seemed disappointed when Rex returned empty-handed.

Parked off the curb, the glistening black cab impeded the flow of traffic, and irate drivers tooted their horns as they navigated around it in the downpour.

"What sort of flowers would you give your fiancée?" Rex asked the man, a fortyish skinhead possessed of a heavy jaw and thick neck.

"Roses, mate."

"Not chrysanthemums?"

The cabby glanced pityingly at him through the sliding partition. " 'Ardly. Them's granny flowers, them is. Where to now, guv? On to Mayfair Mews?"

Rex reconsidered. The rain was coming down hard, and it had been a long day. He gave the driver the address of Wellington House where he was staying.

Dick Whitmore's daughter was an investment banker currently working in Shanghai, and her London apartment was between sub-lets. A cosy studio with a small but well-appointed kitchen, it overlooked a park enclosed by iron railings containing a profusion of horse chestnut trees in full bloom. Rex was ready for the meal prepared and personally delivered by Whitmore's housekeeper, who had already stocked the refrigerator and cupboards with the basic commodities: Milk, tea, bread, biscuits, and jam. He did not plan on wasting time dining in restaurants when he could eat in peace while working on the case. He was due back in court on Monday.

*

The next morning, Rex caught up with Giannelli as he was passing through the cemetery gates after the burial service. He explained he was conducting an inquiry at the behest of Mr. Whitmore, the Howes family solicitor, and begged the fiancé's indulgence at encroaching upon his fresh grief. In point of fact, Gino did not appear overly distressed; more in a hurry to be off. Time was of the essence, Rex explained, since Sir Howes was anxious to locate the driver of the silver car in the absence of any progress made by the Metropolitan Police.

"Perhaps you were escorting Elise home on foot from Presto's and stopped on the way to purchase flowers?" Rex prompted. "In that case, it lets you off suspicion of being behind the wheel."

"I didn't see her," the Italian said with a slight accent, checking his Movedo watch. "And I didn't buy flowers."

Was it possible a handsome foreigner other than Gino had purchased chrysanthemums at Say It with Flowers that same night? On what pretext could he drag Elise's fiancé to the florist for identification by the sales clerk?

"Important engagement?" Rex asked, nodding at the timepiece on the man's darkly matted wrist.

He shrugged in an eloquent manner and gazed at Rex with defiant black eyes. His heavily hooded lids could have given him a sleepy look were he not so tense.

"When did you last see her alive, Mr. Giannelli?"

The Italian sighed. "I told the police all this.

Last Sunday night. She went on a business trip the next day."

"No plans for the following weekend?"

"She was supposed to call me, and never did."

"Doesn't sound like you two were that lovey-dovey." Rex fiddled with the stem of the pipe in his jacket pocket. He'd given up smoking, but still found satisfaction in the familiar smooth feel of the stem and rosewood bowl.

"The wedding was putting a strain on us. She wanted to set a date and I wanted to wait."

"Why was that?"

Again the shrug. "Her father doesn't like me. It made things uncomfortable."

"When did you first hear aboot the accident?" the Scotsman asked.

"Saturday morning. The phone woke me. It was Diana—Lady Howes—in hysterics. Her husband came on the line and said the police would be questioning everyone closely associated with Elise. It sounded like an accusation, which I did not appreciate very much."

Rex could not see any legitimate reason to delay Giannelli further at this point and did not want to overdo his unwelcome. Perhaps more could be gleaned from the alluring and smartly hatted Shannon Smythe, who had peeled away from a group of mourners at the new gravesite slotted in the wet grass.

"Miss Smythe, my name is Rex Graves, QC," he said as he approached on the path and held out his hand.

"I know who you are," she said taking it. "I saw you yesterday at the funeral parlour." Emerald eyes, green as the grass and accentuated by a glossy black brim, appraised him with frank interest. "Mr. Whitmore said you had questions about Elise's whereabouts on Friday night." Her voice was fashionable young London, imbued with an appealing huskiness.

"Aye, and I hope you'll be kind enough to answer them. Did you know of any plans Elise might have had? I realize you've already gone through all this with the police, but there's a gap in the timeline."

"I have no idea what her plans were. She was working late Friday catching up after her trip to Paris. Her door was closed. I left the office around six. We didn't typically see each other at weekends, except professionally."

"Why was that?" Drops of rain began to fall, and Rex opened his brolly in an attempt to shield the young woman in her black silk suit and hat.

"We had our own sets of friends.

"But you were chummy in college."

"True. But then Elise started seeing Gino, and I really don't care for him and his playboy crowd. It was obvious he was using her for her money."

"In what way?"

"Only last week he hit her up for a large loan for his car import business."

"Her own private money?"

"Yes, but capital that could have been invested in Head Start! to develop our line in handbags and other accessories. Naturally, I was opposed, but Jennifer told her sister the loan was a sound investment, and Elise listened. Jenn only said that to butter Gino up, who it's obvious she has the hots for."

"I take it you dislike Jennifer?" Rex inferred from her disdainful tone.

"She likes to snoop and cause trouble."

"Give me a for instance."

Standing close to him under the brolly, Shannon Smythe gazed up at him with a gleam of amusement in her fine eyes. "You are very persistent, Mr. Graves. Well, all right then. When I stayed at the Howes' home one time when Elise and I were students, Jenn caught us sneaking out late to go to a club. She told Sir Howes, who's a strict old bugger, as you probably know. Jenn has always been jealous of her sister having loads more boyfriends. And she was positively green over Gino."

"I thought Jennifer was looking for a rich husband," Rex asked disingenuously, aware of the looks of longing Jennifer had cast in Giannelli's direction at the funeral home.

"Gino's doing all right for himself. He was expanding his business. Hence the loan."

"I hear your business was on the up and up too."

"Elise and I made a good team. I took care of the merchandising, she had the flair and the contacts. My own family is not rich and connected," Shannon stated.

"What will you do now?" Rex switched the brolly to his other arm to relieve his aching muscles. He had hoped for some mellow May sunshine for his trip south.

"Now I'll have to hire a new designer." Shannon chewed on her lip, looking in that moment more like a schoolgirl than a London sophisticate. "Look, I have to go, but you can come by my office anytime." She pulled a business card from her black suede handbag, declining his offer to escort her to her car.

Rex watched as her high heels propelled her around puddles to the zippy Fiat 500 Cabrio parked at the curb. Not exactly a sports car, as defined by the nightclub witness, but silver grey nonetheless. And how reliable had his account been, after all? Presumably he'd had a few drinks that night.

Rex decided to dig around some more, proceeding with the chauffeur.

Erik Christiansen was waiting by the silver

stretch limo, taut as steel and professionally impervious to the rain, his black cap dripping onto the darkening shoulders of his black uniform. Rex approached, anticipating a frosty reception, and was not disabused. Christiansen claimed to know nothing about the hit-and- run and little about the personal affairs of the family. He merely drove the various members about town and occasionally into neighbouring counties to visit friends at their country estates. Unlike the melodious intonations of Gino Giannelli, he spoke flawless, almost unaccented English, interspersed with the occasional Americanism. An experienced Crown prosecutor, Rex felt certain Christiansen knew more than he was telling. The words sounded rehearsed, the pale eyes veered from his own or else held them too long. At that moment, Sir Howes appeared at the gate with his wife, his remaining daughter, and the relic aunts. Christiansen took off toward them with a golf umbrella, leaving Rex to plan his next move. Lunch.

*

Presto's proved to be more illuminating this time around, once Rex circumvented the tight-lipped wait staff and convinced the behind-the-scenes employees he was not from the police. He discovered that the head chef, when adequately compensated for the information, had a cousin who was a house agent, and said cousin had sublet a body repair shop to "GiGi," as Gino Giannelli was affectionately known at the bistro. Most of the employees were from the same region in Southern Italy as GiGi, if not the same town, and "took care" of their own. Yet they would sell their grandmother for a big enough bribe, Rex ruminated as he left the premises with a considerably lighter wallet—and the name of the property agent in Soho.

Next, he made his way to Elise's home on foot and arrived at a late Georgian building split into ten flats and serviced by a porter wearing a waistcoat. Doubtless apprised by Sir Howes or Mr. Whitmore of Rex's business, the elderly man let him into number five without a murmur of protest. Here Rex found Jennifer dressed in slacks and a puce angora sweater sifting through a morass of papers and photos in the front drawing room. Joining her on the white leather sectional, Rex told her his business and apologized for the imposition.

"You're the Scottish barrister who solved the murders at Swanmere Manor."

"Among others."

"And you're hoping to find the hit-and-run driver?"

"If at all possible."

"Could be anyone. London is a big place."

"Well, I know *that*. But your father feels it was closer to home, so to speak. Call it paternal instinct." Or paranoia.

Jennifer drew her inelegant legs beneath her chin. Her bare feet were bereft of nail varnish, just as her face was nude of visible makeup. Rex reflected once more on the vagaries of genetics. And yet her equine features were not unattractive in a singularly British way.

"Looking for anything in particular?" he asked, cocking his head at the pile of papers between them on the plush sofa.

"Just private stuff my sister wouldn't have wanted anybody to see. I just want to protect her."

"You two were close?"

"Oh, yes. We never had any secrets."

However, Jennifer admitted to having no clue as to why Elise had gone to Presto's unless it was to meet Gino. The phone conversation with her sister on Friday afternoon had concerned a family brunch the next day at Claridge's, a monthly event organized by the decrepit aunts, and which the girls attended in hopes of a sizeable inheritance, being the sole viable heirs.

"Do you have a job, Miss Howes?" Rex asked.

She regarded him blankly. "I have my allowance and still live at home, but I'm staying here for a few days to sort out Elise's things. I do a lot of charity work, of course. Mummy's very much into that sort of thing. It's the duty of the privileged class, she says, and of a politician's wife. And why take a job away from someone who actually needs it? Elise only got into business because she couldn't find any hats she really liked. She always was rather artistic. I'm the practical one."

Rex smiled in spite of himself. He felt he might get somewhere with Jennifer Howes. She came across as earnest and eager to please. "I gather Shannon Smythe is the practical one in your sister's enterprise."

"I suppose so. Elise could never have managed without her. No head for figures *at all!*"

"And Shannon has, I take it."

"Oh, yes. She helped sort out Gino's taxes, which were a dreadful mess."

"I thought Shannon didn't like Elise's fiancé." Rex saw no reason not to stir the pot a little. Ms. Smythe had made it clear the two women did not care for each other.

Jennifer smirked. "Shows how little *you* know. I saw a bouquet of red roses on her desk. Two dozen." She paused for dramatic effect. "They were from him."

"From Gino?" The girl nodded. "Was there a card?" he asked.

"Yes, and it said, '*Your devoted Gino.*' I just happened to notice." The young woman had the decency to blush.

"Did Elise know aboot this?"

"Unlikely. She was out of town that week."

"Ah."

The roses struck a discordant note in his mind. Had Shannon lied to him about her feelings for Gino? Most women, in his prosaic experience, while perhaps loath to consign a lavish bouquet of roses to the bin, would nonetheless discard the note of an unwelcome admirer. And if Shannon liked him so little, why had she helped with his finances? As a favour to Elise? Very puzzling, he thought. One thing to ponder, however: Gino could be a man who said it—whatever the occasion—with flowers.

"Did he ever give you flowers?"

Jennifer's hand went to her throat and fingered a string of pearls. "Me? Why?"

"I heard he received a loan from your sister for his luxury car venture. Thanks in part to you."

"That's right. She wrote out a cheque to him for fifty thousand pounds."

"When was this exactly?"

"This past Friday, according to this counterfoil." She showed it to Rex.

"Funny. I spoke to Gino and he said he hadn't seen Elise since Sunday of the week before."

"He might have picked it up from the receptionist. Elise had a hair appointment Friday afternoon, so he might have missed her."

"Aye, perhaps. One more thing, Miss Howes. Do you drive?"

"Yes, sort of. I mean, I have my learner's permit."

After thanking Jennifer for her cooperation, Rex took his leave with parting words of solace, though he knew from experience how inadequate such words could be, having lost his wife to breast cancer when his son was fifteen.

He decided, in light of Jennifer's revelation, to take up Ms. Smythe's invitation. Thanking a woman with a large bouquet of red roses for helping with one's taxes seemed to Rex an extravagant, even romantic, gesture. Retrieving the business card Shannon had given him, he arranged to meet with the *modiste* at her office suite, located in Park Lane close to where he was staying.

A cheery yellow sofa welcomed visitors to the second-floor lobby of Head Start!, where a collection of headpieces displayed on tall stands provided further flourishes of colour and texture, and offset the concept of works of art in themselves. Several were adorned with exotic feathery plumes, realistic peppermint candy canes, and glass cocktail twizzlers, frivolous affairs in Rex's opinion. He reflected it would take a very confident woman to wear some of these fantastical creations perched on her person, although they might look not out of place on a Milan or Paris runway. As he examined them, he looked for price tags, curious as to what the cost of high fashion might be...

"Mr. Graves?" enquired a skirt-suited young woman stepping into the room. "Shannon will see you now."

Pivoting in the direction whence she had come, she led the way to her employer's office. Declining Ms. Smythe's offer of a cappuccino, Rex settled into one of two comfortable bucket armchairs across from her desk and came straight to the point.

"Miss Smythe, may I ask—do you have a special young man in your life?"

The fulsome young woman, who had changed out of mourning, blushed beneath her crimson beret. "I don't." She laughed unconvincingly. "Where would I find the time?"

"Cards on the table, Miss Smythe. Gino declared his devotion to you with roses, did he not?"

Shannon blushed more alarmingly now, almost matching the hue of her felt cap. "That's only because I helped him with his taxes."

"If I may be so bold, you remind me of a young Sophia Loren, and I'm sure your charms are not lost on a hot-blooded Italian."

"Wow. You're not one to beat about the

bush!" Shannon chewed on her fingernail while Rex waited patiently for an admission he was sure was forthcoming. She struck him as basically a straightforward young woman. "Oh, why am I protecting the wanker?" she said at length. Sitting back in her executive chair, she took a shuddering breath. "Yes, I was having a sordid fling with Gino. And you cannot imagine the guilt I feel, especially now, with Elise dead. Some friend *I* turned out to be," she added.

"You were with him Friday night?"

"I was. And yes, I lied to the police about staying home giving myself a pedicure. I knew he was meeting Elise for a late dinner, but we got carried away."

"He finally went off to meet her? On foot?"

Shannon nodded and looked at him full-on across the desk. "And I'll tell you this much. I saw him pocket a container of pills as he was getting dressed. A full container, mind. When I asked what they were for, he said they were aspirin for his headache. He had certainly not been complaining of a headache just minutes before."

"What do you think the pills were?"

"XTC, I'm sure of it. He'd tried to get me to take it once at a party, and I recognized the bottle, which is a regular aspirin bottle. He'd got Elise hooked. I could tell he was lying about a headache, but it was like he didn't care if I knew he was lying or not."

Rex asked himself whether drugs had been found in Elise's system, and, if so, that fact had been hushed up. Dick Whitmore had only told him about her alcohol intake. "You think he planned to drug Elise?" he asked. "Why?"

Shannon swivelled this way and that in her chair. "She intended to cancel the cheque for the loan. I think that snitch of a sister told her about the roses Gino sent me."

Perhaps this information had been imparted during the Friday afternoon phone conversation with Jennifer. Being stood up at the bistro was probably the clincher for Elise, and she had confronted her fiancé. That same night she was killed in a hit-and-run just steps from her home. Mere coincidence?

"Did you tell him Elise was going to cancel the fifty thousand pounds?"

"He already knew. I wouldn't have told him, in any case. He has a filthy temper."

"Then you most definitely should stay away from him," Rex said in a fatherly tone.

"I know. I don't even like him. He's just so bloody hard to resist."

"Resist," he told her in no uncertain terms, warming his words with a smile.

Eyes downcast, Shannon murmured resolutely that she would.

Now, Rex thought; who had told Gino about Elise's decision to cancel the cheque? Three guesses it was Jennifer, trying again to get on his good side—if, in fact, he had one. After some delay getting her phone number, and a good deal of prevaricating on her part, he was able to ascertain that she had indeed warned Gino and had told Elise about the roses. He deduced this last act had been out of jealousy and spite.

Postponing his dinner plans, Rex made for Sloane Car Service to pursue his conversation with Erik Christiansen, which had been curtailed that morning at the cemetery. After the interview he would head back to Wellington House and see what Mr. Whitmore's housekeeper had prepared for his dinner. His last meal, a savoury steak and kidney pie coiffed in flaky pastry, had been accompanied by a bottle of rather good claret. Ignoring the rumblings in his stomach, he pursued his destination. Business before pleasure, he reminded himself, especially when the business was murder.

*

He found Erik Christiansen in a subterranean garage lined with luxury sedans polishing the chrome on the silver limo. Dressed in black livery, he straightened when he saw Rex. He was about two inches shy of the older man's six-four without his cap, which hung from the hood ornament.

"Tell me what you know," Rex urged the Howes' family chauffeur, sensing that a direct plea would elicit more confidence than a bribe. "I sense there's something more than you let on earlier."

"I really don't know anything. And I don't want to lose my best client."

"Sir Howes is the one who retained my services, so we're working for the same person. Anything you can tell me that relates to his dead daughter, however insignificant it may have appeared to you at the time, would be appreciated. And, hopefully, helpful in finding the driver who knocked her down."

With a brief look around the garage, Christiansen nodded. "But just so you understand, this is a good gig and I don't want to lose it."

"Understood."

"So, Friday night, I dropped her parents off at a dinner in Mayfair and was cruising around looking for a place to eat, when I saw her leave Presto's. I stopped the car and she got in. She said she'd been stood up."

"By Gino?"

"Yeah. She was close to tears, but more angry, you know? I tried to comfort her."

"And how did you do that?" The icy Christiansen did not strike Rex as the hugging, soothing type.

"I kissed her. She kissed me back. She was tipsy, that's for sure. We kissed for a while. It seemed to make her feel better. Don't tell Sir Howes any of this. She told me she was going to break off the engagement with Gino. Pride had prevented her from calling him to find out where he was, and sometimes he didn't answer her calls. I thought this strange. Gino was on to a good thing. Why screw up? Elise was rich and beautiful, with a powerful father. Anyway, she finally told me to let her out of the car. She wanted to walk home."

"Did she walk in that direction, or in the opposite direction towards Gino's place?"

"Towards her place. I insisted she let me drive her. Her father would have wanted me to. I mean, she was in no state...but she said the air would do her good."

"She had no flowers with her at that point?"

"Flowers? No. Just a handbag."

"Mr. Christiansen, how long have you been driving the Howes?"

"Eight, nine months."

"Have you been in London long?"

"Long enough to know my way around."

"Essential in your line of work, I imagine. Is this your only line of work?"

Christiansen flushed pink beneath his pale skin. "I'm training for the stage. I lived in L.A. for a time doing the valet-acting thing, but I thought I might get further if I came here to study as a Shakespearean actor. I hope to get into the RSC and perhaps go back to the States later."

Rex wished him good luck and said he'd make a good Hamlet. The Dane gave the faintest of smiles and got back to his task of sprucing up the limo.

"By the way, do you know where the Italian Ambassador lives?" Rex asked over his shoulder. "It would save me time looking it up."

Christiansen straightened his lean frame, the polishing cloth dangling from his right hand. "Of course. He's a friend of Sir Howes. He was the guest of honour at the club party that night." He gave Rex the address.

*

Rex waited in line at the coffee house across the street from his borrowed flat. Done out in shades of brown and beige, with a framed floor-to-ceiling mirror behind the polished wood counter, the café exuded a fragrance of French custard and the aroma of freshly ground coffee beans. He ordered a latte and two pastries, and took his breakfast into the park.

A solitary green bench in a corner beckoned among the copper beech, oak, and horse chestnut trees. He sat enjoying the watery sunshine, while drifts of creamy white blossoms ruffled in the breeze at his feet, and savoured the moment along with his breakfast before making his first in-person call of the day.

The previous night after dinner he had spread his notes across the living room table and moved the angle poise lamp from the small desk. He had worked for a while in the pool of light, making annotations and studying photos of the scene of the accident. Then, chewing on his dry pipe as he contemplated the framed posters on the wall depicting red maple leaves in autumnal Beijing, he had considered likely scenarios relating to the hit-and-run, based on the facts supplied by Mr. Whitmore and on his own information. One stood out. Abruptly he had left his work on the table and gone out on a clandestine mission.

He now watched in distraction while a dishevelled old woman, the front buttons on her tweed coat misaligned, rolled a shopping bag made of stiff tartan cloth along the diagonal path through the park. The material bulged with elongated cylindrical shapes. Rex was in no doubt as to what the zipped-up bag contained. Whatever the lady's alcoholic preference, she appeared eager to get home to consume it and proceeded at a purposeful clip. Would Elise Howes, with her predilection for drink, have ended up the same way? he wondered.

A sudden gust ripped through the trees sending a new shower of woodsy- scented chestnut blooms onto the grass. Retrieving his black brolly, he rose from the bench. He discarded the coffee container and pastry box in a corrugated iron bin, and exited the park. On the street he hailed a black cab, giving the driver the Italian Ambassador's address.

Vittorio Scalfaro was home, confined to a day bed in the drawing room with a professed migraine, and draped in a silk robe of midnight blue. He was almost comically flabbergasted when the Scotsman told him he had found his silver Ferrari in Giannelli's "other" garage undergoing a touch-up.

"You found my stolen car?"

Judging by the decor, the ambassador was a man of refined taste, and Rex felt frumpy by comparison. But Scalfaro was not a good liar, at least not for a diplomat.

"Not stolen, Ambassador," Rex said pointedly. "Merely temporarily out of commission. Your private club gave me a list of the valet-parked cars for Friday night. Yours was returned to you withoot a scratch shortly before Miss Howes' accident."

The man's clean-shaven face sank into blurred lines. Rex decided to cut him some slack. Scalfaro appeared to be suffering enough.

"You probably did not see the young woman step out onto the street. A van blocked your visibility, and it was dark. Had the wheel been on the right-hand side, you might have seen her sooner and had a chance to break."

"Alas, so true!" The ambassador spoke in melodious tones, like Gino's. "I should have bought a car with British steering, but I planned on driving the Ferrari back to Italy. Signorina Howes leapt out of nowhere! I felt the impact and took off in a blind panic. I didn't realize at the time that the pedestrian was Sir Howes' daughter. I thought I should get home right away and seek legal advice. After all, a person in my position... How would it look?"

"Worse now," Rex informed him. "The police will suspect you of drinking. And charge you with fleeing the scene of an accident."

Scalfaro raised his hands in supplication. "A gin and tonic and two glasses of wine with dinner. It is conceivable I was going too fast—one always does in Ferraris, but traffic was light. I am filled with remorse. But, what can be proved?"

Not a lot, Rex thought; except that the man was a coward. To top it all, he had diplomatic immunity from prosecution. What, he enquired out of interest, had Scalfaro's legal advice been?

"To wait on events. When no one was able to

identify my car, my attorney suggested I get it fixed without delay using the utmost discretion. The repercussions as Italian Ambassador to the UK could be embarrassing in the extreme, and Parliament has enough embarrassment to deal with. If only I could turn back the clock of that terrible night!" Scalfaro lamented.

Aye, thought Rex, but the girl would probably be dead anyhow, at Giannelli's hands.

And what did Rex plan to do with this information? the ambassador asked, rising shakily from the Victorian day bed.

"Not my decision," Rex told him, excusing himself with a curt goodbye.

It was time to confront Gino Giannelli.

*

Rex consulted his notebook for the business address Mr. Whitmore had provided, and availed himself of the waiting cab. A shower broke out as they took off down the quiet leafy street and turned onto a thoroughfare. Rex sat back on the worn seat and re-ordered his thoughts. Getting some sort of confession or at least confirmation of his hypothesis from Elise's fiancé would be crucial to wrapping up the case.

"But the police searched my premises." The young Italian spread his arms wide, indicating the breadth of hangar filled with a half dozen imported luxury cars. He gestured impatiently to a mechanic to leave them. The place was immaculate, the smell of new tires and engine oil intoxicating. Rex who, incongruously for his size, drove an economical Mini Cooper, found himself seduced by the sleek long bonnets and sexy rear ends of these gas-hungry predators. Gino caressed the moulded front quarter panel of a cherry red Maserati GranTurismo with almost sensual pleasure. Clearly these machines were his passion.

"I was referring to a body shop which you omitted to tell the detectives aboot," Rex enlightened him. "I saw a freshly sprayed silver Ferrari in there." He had shinnied up a drainpipe the previous night with a pocket torch, a precarious endeavour considering his bulk, but in the pursuit of justice worth the risk of a broken ankle.

"So?"

"It made me curious and more than a little suspicious, especially when I saw the diplomatic plate. I traced it back to a Vittorio Scalfaro whom you sold it to in March. Your personal assistant was very helpful when I called this morning posing as a potential buyer. As was the house agent who found you the new premises." And Mr. Whitmore, of course. The solicitor had identified the Ferrari as belonging to the Italian Ambassador, a friend of Sir

Howes'.

"Your point?" Gino demanded, showing impatience.

"The ambassador came to you for a repair job—a little *quid pro quo*."

"What do you mean?"

"He'd been dining in Mayfair and left the club shortly before the accident, in which he has admitted his involvement. Perhaps he saw you at the scene."

"He didn't. Nobody saw me." Gino fell silent, realizing his error. His hand struck the two-door coupé he'd been fondling. "*Merda!*" he swore.

"Say It with Flowers stays open late at the weekend. The girl at the shop told me a man fitting your description paid cash for a bunch of chrysanthemums just before closing. Mums?" Rex asked emphatically, raising an eyebrow.

"They were a peace offering for being late," Gino explained—warily.

"Roses are more romantic, not so?"

"The roses were drooping and sad. I liked the look of the golden balls. So sunny, so alive! I got them on the way to her place."

"Spur of the moment?"

"That is how I am. Impulsive. They told me at Presto's she had left not long before. I saw her on the street and called out her name."

"What then?"

"I explained I had overslept from a nap and was coming over to her flat to surprise her. I offered to walk her home, but she was having none of it. She was angry, and a little drunk. She only accepted the flowers when I threatened to throw them in the gutter. The next thing that happened was an accident. She stepped into the road still shouting at me over her shoulder. The driver took off in a hurry, and I couldn't make out the number plate. It happened so fast."

Giannelli mopped his brow with the cuff of his spotless blue overalls. "I knew Elise's father would blame me, even though it wasn't my fault, so I left when I saw another person coming to her aid." Rex felt sure he would have fled anyway. "Later, when Vittorio dropped off his Ferrari, I had my suspicions. A yellow petal was stuck in the grille."

"But you couldn't be sure he hadn't seen you, so you did the repair, no questions asked."

Giannelli made no reply.

"The good Samaritan heard Elise say 'Chris' and 'Jean' with her dying breath. I suspect she was trying to say "chrysanthemums" and managed the first part of your name, Gin-o. The chrysanthemum in your country represents death. The flowers you gave her were a death warning. Not true?" A sous-chef at Presto's had supplied this interesting titbit when Rex asked if chrysanthemums were popular in Italy, thus confirming what his suicidal ex-girlfriend had told him.

Gino shook his head derisively, going so far as to tap his temple to indicate the Scotsman's lack of sanity. "You are reading too much into all of this."

Undeterred, Rex continued his theory. "You heard the powerful engine of a speeding car and pushed Elise in front of it, not realizing it was Scalfaro's Ferrari. The left-hand drive may have afforded the ambassador less reaction time as Elise 'leapt' onto the street, as he described it. A wee push by you in her inebriated state would have sufficed."

"*Vaffanculo!*" Dark fire flashed in Gino's eyes. While Rex did not understand what had just been said, it sounded obscene nonetheless. "Why would I want to kill her?"

"Several reasons. First, you saw her in the limo with Christiansen and got jealous."

"I admit I saw her with the chauffeur, but she got out soon afterwards, and I followed."

"Even though you were cheating on Elise, you didn't like seeing her kiss another man. But you had planned to kill her anyway, before she could cancel the cheque for your business. Hence the Ecstasy, which Shannon saw you take with you and which you would have rammed down Elise's throat once you got her home, and then made it look like suicide. But she blew you off on the street, and her indiscretion with the Dane served to add fuel to the fire. You saw another opportunity for murder when that Ferrari came tearing down the road. Impulsive and spur of the moment," Rex added with a mirthless smile. "Is that not how you described yourself?"

"You can't prove any of this!" Giannelli said, echoing his compatriot.

Maybe not, Rex thought grimly. It was all circumstantial, but the accusations had certainly got the wind up the hot-headed Italian. And he wouldn't be giving Shannon any more roses.

*

Rex called the solicitor upon leaving Gino's garage and made an appointment to report his findings.

"Premeditated murder is not easy to prove in this case," Rex concluded at Mr. Whitmore's office. The solicitor sitting at his desk was a fussy little man with womanish hands. "Giannelli caught a lucky break if his intention was to O.D. his fiancée. A reckless driver beat him to the punch, with perhaps a little help from Casanova. Elise Howes was drunk and probably distracted to-boot, so it was a perfect opportunity. Pure coincidence it was one of Giannelli's cars."

"Ye-es," Mr. Whitmore said ruminatively. The tapered fingers, on which glinted a bejewelled wedding ring, drummed the mahogany surface of the antique partners' desk. "Well, we had better just stick to the facts. Sir Howes can draw his own conclusions. It won't be the news he anticipated, of course. What a devastating thing to have happen. Vittorio Scalfaro's reputation will be ruined if this gets out. However, that Sir Howes' prospective son-in-law was cheating on his daughter will come as no surprise. But I would have credited Shannon with more sense." The solicitor checked his gold Rolex and grabbed a hat and umbrella from the coat tree behind his door. "Sir Howes is expecting us. There's a car waiting outside."

The cabinet minister resided at Wilton Crescent in a grand terrace house five stories high, a frill of black iron balconies adorning the stone clad façade. He received his guests once again in the rich wood-panelled library and offered them sherry, barely able to disguise his displeasure when he heard the results of Rex's investigation. It soon became clear he intended to make public Vittorio Scalfaro's involvement in his daughter's death.

"What a can of worms," he growled, turning to Rex. "And Giannelli sold him that Ferrari. Bloody stupid, if you ask me, bombing around in one of those dangerous toys. And then my future son-in-law left my little girl to die on the street. He might've well have just killed her himself."

Rex privately concurred.

*

Several weeks later at his chambers in Edinburgh, Rex received a call from Mr. Whitmore to the effect that Gino Giannelli had overdosed on Ecstasy. He had been found by his cleaning lady drowned in his bathtub, naked among a sprinkling of floating petals. A card in Italian found on the tile floor, and subsequently leaked to the press, thanked Gino for making the sender's time in London more pleasurable; however, in view of Gino's past connection with the Howes family and the "unfortunate accident," the flowers were being sent not only as a token of tender affection but of regretful adieu. Signed, "Vitto."

There existed no possibility in Rex's mind that a lovelorn Gino had committed suicide, still less that he was homosexual, as the message and flowers insinuated. The Italian Ambassador had vehemently denied sending either, as, in the mind of the public, he would. Rex could not suppress a wry smile of appreciation at the apt and subtle revenge exacted on Gino and Vittorio Scalfaro. "A curiously Shakespearean concept," he remarked to Mr. Whitmore, reflecting on the watery grave and ironic floral touch.

"Quite," replied the Howes family solicitor, adding that his client had made it quite clear that he did not require Rex's assistance in this particular case.

"Mum's the word," the Scotsman acknowledged, appropriately, he thought.

However, as a man of the law, he felt somewhat conflicted.

Apparently Sir Howes, with the aid of his loyal Danish factotum, had prescribed justice to his full satisfaction.

BOOKS IN THE REX GRAVES MYSTERY SERIES:

Christmas Is Murder

Starred Review from *Booklist:*

The first installment in this new mystery series is a winner. The amateur detective is Rex Graves, a Scottish barrister, fond of Sudoku puzzles and Latin quotations. In an old-fashioned conceit, Challinor begins with a cast of characters, along with hints of possible motives for each. Although set firmly in the present, this tale reads like a classic country-house mystery. Rex and the others are snowed in at the Swanmere Manor hotel in East Sussex, England. Being the last to arrive, Rex immediately hears of the unexpected demise of one of the other guests. By the time the police arrive days later, additional bodies have piled up and motives are rampant, but Rex has identified the murderer. At times, it seems we are playing Clue or perhaps enjoying a contemporary retelling of a classic Agatha Christie tale *(And Then There Were None,* or *At Bertram's Hotel)* with a charming new sleuth. A must for cozy fans.

Murder in the Raw

Mystery Scene Magazine:

In *Murder in the Raw*, Scottish barrister Rex Graves must expose—and I do mean expose—the killer of Sabine Durand, a French actress who goes missing one evening from a nudist resort in the Caribbean... Set on an island, *Murder in the Raw* is a clever variant on the locked room mystery, and Rex discovers that everyone in this self-contained locale has a secret when it comes to the intriguing Sabine. Who, though, would benefit from her disappearance or murder? With a host of colorful characters, a dose of humor and a balmy locale, you will want to devour this well-plotted mystery. I won't spoil your pleasure by divulging the solution, but suffice it to say that Challinor provides a most compelling answer.

Phi Beta Murder*

Foreword Magazine:

Readers meet up once again with Rex Graves in
the third mystery to follow the Scottish barrister
with a knack for getting involved in the ultimate
crime. Rex is on his way out of the beautiful
Scottish countryside leaving behind Helen, his new
woman friend and his mother to visit his son on
the campus of his American college. Campbell
Graves is supposed to be enjoying life at Hilliard
University in Jacksonville, Florida, but lately on the
phone he's sounded rather distant, and Rex wants
nothing more than to see his son and make sure
everything is all right. Unfortunately the day he
steps on campus is the day a young man is found
in his locked room hanging from the ceiling. Soon
Rex must split his time between worrying about his
son, solving a crime that seems to involve a million
people with a million different agendas, and trying
to balance his love life without losing people in the
process. Humor and well-written characters add to
the story, as does some reflection on the causes of
suicide. A wonderful read and great plot for cozy

mystery lovers.

This title has not been endorsed by the Phi Beta Kappa Society. The Phi Beta Kappa fraternity depicted in the novel is in no way affiliated nor associated with the Phi Beta Kappa Society.

Murder on the Moor

BellaOnline:

Scottish Barrister and amateur sleuth Rex Graves purchased Gleneagle Lodge so that he and his girlfriend, Helen D'Arcy, could get away to spend some private time together. Now he wonders why he had agreed to host a housewarming party. When one of the guests turns up dead, her body found in a nearby loch, the finger-pointing begins. Graves cannot help but put his sleuthing skills to work as he tries to find out who killed his house guest while he also gathers clues as to who is committing the so-called Moor Murders. He is wondering if the two are tied and if he is hosting the killer. When a storm prevents anyone from leaving, Rex and Helen do their best to keep everyone calm during their forced confinement. Set in the Scottish Highlands, Challinor successfully utilizes the atmosphere of the countryside to enhance the tension going on inside the Lodge. The characters seem typical of the type seen in many mysteries written by such authors as Agatha Christie, and are a welcome diversion from today's style of writing. The writing is crisp and the story fast-paced. The inevitable gathering of the guests in the library comes with a twist or two, and the ending is a satisfying conclusion to a solid whodunit.

Murder of the Bride

Buried Under Books:

Rex Graves is back, this time visiting his fiancée, Helen d'Arcy, so they can attend the wedding in Aston-on-Trent of one of her former students. Polly Newcombe is very pregnant and her groom, Timmy Thorpe looks a bit peaked, but is it just the dreary day leading Rex to think the success of this marriage is doubtful? Perhaps not, as the reception at the bride's family country home in Derbyshire soon turns from a pleasant celebration to a scene of mayhem when Polly collapses, looking more than a little green. Leaving the reception and heading to Aston-on-Trent, Rex learns a great deal more about the secrets of the Newcombe and Thorpe families. Is jealousy behind the attacks? Greed? Infidelity? Overbearing mothers? Rex and the local police have an overabundance of clues and evidence, and getting to the solution to the case will require much thought and cooperation. This latest case for Rex Graves is every bit as charming and entertaining as those in earlier books and readers will not be disappointed. The setting, an English country home, is as much a character as the people, and many of those characters are a delight, especially Police Constable Perrin (and the cast of characters provided by the author is very much appreciated).

Murder at the Dolphin Inn

Cozy Mystery Book Reviews:

Scottish barrister, Rex Graves, and his fiancée are on a cruise to Mexico. When they disembark at Key West, Florida, they hear of a bizarre story surrounding the local B&B. The owners, Merle and Taffy Dyer, were killed during the Key West's October Fantasy Fest. Rex can't resist a mystery and can't wait to abandon the cruise and dive head first into solving this mystery. It's going to take all of Rex's sleuthing skills to find out who out of all the seemingly innocent family and friends killed the owners. The premise of this mystery reminds me of the traditional mysteries I read in my teens. It is very much reminiscent of M.C. Beaton and Agatha Christie, with a quaint inn and a sleuth determined to find the truth. From their first discovering of the murders to the final revealing of the murderer, Rex and Helen are an outstanding sleuthing duo. They reminded me so much of Agatha Christie's Tommy and Tuppence, hunting down clues and uncovering killers. With numerous twists and turns, *Murder at the Dolphin Inn* provides a first class whodunit, and I absolutely can't wait to find out what adventure Rex and Helen go on next.

Murder at Midnight

Booklist:

On a stormy New Year's Eve, Rex Graves, an Edinburgh barrister, and his fiancée, Helen d'Arcy, are hosting a Hogmanay gathering at his Highlands retreat, hopeful that this party will be uneventful, unlike the housewarming last summer that ended with murder. All seems to be well, with the Frasers explaining the legal maneuverings undertaken to reclaim their family history and cement their right to Gleneagle Castle, the estate next door, and their certainty that Jacobite treasure will be found in the ruins of the Keep. Then, with a stormy crash, the lights go out. As the party regroups, they discover that the Frasers are dead. While they await the arrival of the police—and the electric company—Rex leads the discussion about how the deaths might have occurred. Once Chief Inspector Dalgerry arrives, the investigation begins in earnest. The sixth in the series, this is a classic country-house mystery, with modern day twists and turns adding to the fun.

Murder Comes Calling

Available for pre-order; release August 2015:

Who's at the door? Best not answer with a killer at large in the neighbourhood. When a spate of murders takes place in the quiet riverfront community of Notting Hamlet in south-central England, Rex Graves is called upon to lend his investigatory expertise. So far, four residents have perished in their homes, apparently at the hands of a sadistic serial killer. The only obvious link among the victims is that they all had their homes up for sale. The local constabulary have detained a shady house agent, but letters written in blood on the bodies tip the Scottish barrister off to an altogether different kind of killer. For the first time in his sleuthing career, Rex finds he is not up against a lone operator and has good reason to fear for his life.

ABOUT THE AUTHOR

C.S. Challinor was born in Bloomington, Indiana, and raised and educated in both Scotland and England. She now lives in Southwest Florida.

Visit the author at *www.rexgraves.com*